To Cookie
from
Peter

CINCHFOOT

THOMAS C. HINKLE

CINCHFOOT

The Story of a Range Horse

GROSSET & DUNLAP

Publishers, New York

TO THE MEMORY OF A GREAT HORSE

Author's Note

CINCHFOOT and Blaze Face, under different
names, are based on real characters. The re-
markable friendship between them was a re-
ality. Horsemen of the West, including Lloyd
Hardin and John Campbell, have more than
once told me of the two horses and their unusual friendship for each other. Nor was this
the only incident in the West when a gelding
befriended a small colt and a friendship
sprang up between the two that lasted
throughout life.

When Cinchfoot was last heard of he was
twenty-three years old, living on a ranch in
Montana. It was said by those who saw him
at the time that he was in excellent health and
as beautiful as ever. Old Blaze Face lived to
be twenty-six years of age before he crossed
the Great Divide.

T. C. H.

Contents

CINCHFOOT

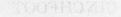

I: *Cinchfoot*

THE day had suddenly turned dark as night, as one of the worst rain storms of the West roared across the open valley. The small herd of range horses ran with all their might before the driving wind and rain. They were led by a big black gelding with a white face, known as Blaze Face. Close on the heels of this big leader ran a yearling colt, destined to be known as Cinchfoot. He was of a striking color, being coal black with white, or what was called silver, mane and tail. It is true he did not as yet have much mane and tail, but it was growing and he was already big for a yearling. It was plain enough, also, that he could run. Blaze Face led all the others, but Cinchfoot had no trouble keeping up. He was right on the heels of the big horse and it seemed to him they should go faster still. Here and there, as the lightning glared, stood tall pine trees, their branches moving and battling with the driving storm. Frequently deafening crashes of thunder sounded, and as the horses rushed past the scattering timber, a tall pine was struck and knocked into splinters by a lurid streak of fire. It was a storm of unusual severity for this time of the year.

Suddenly, only a few yards ahead, a glaring bolt of lightning struck the ground, making the earth quiver and tremble. A deafening blast followed and the horses were almost knocked down. They stopped suddenly, the big gelding, Blaze Face, going back on his haunches in the effort. Cinchfoot also stopped suddenly and in the blackness that followed he felt a pain in his head and small stars seemed to be glimmering before his eyes.

He and all the other horses were dazed, but the cold rain pelting down on them brought them to their senses. Blaze Face leaped forward again, trying to find shelter from the driving rain, and they all followed. He had led them but a short distance when another blinding flash of lightning showed him he was almost on the verge of a river at the flood. A cloudburst had fallen upstream and the river rushed down madly at this point, its banks overflowing. Had the horses run into the river here the seething torrent would have picked them up like so many corks and carried them down between the high rocky walls where they would all have been drowned. Blaze Face stopped, then in the black darkness that followed the blinding flash, he turned and ran eastward through the driving sheets of rain. But again he stopped suddenly. The river made a sharp turn here and again he had stopped the range horses just in time. This time Blaze Face whirled and led his small band of followers for some distance into the face of the storm, when he stopped and turned his tail toward the driving wind and rain. The other horses all clustered around him, including the yearling colt, Cinchfoot. He stood close against Blaze Face. In fact he was always close to the big gelding. As the two stood here, side by side, Blaze Face put his nose to Cinchfoot's and in some way let him know they would have to stay here and "take it." This was enough for Cinchfoot. From the time the colt was very small Blaze Face had taken a strange liking to him and when Cinchfoot's mother stumbled into a badger hole one day and broke her leg, dying where she fell, Blaze Face took the whole responsibility of looking after the little colt. Cinchfoot was hardly three months old when the accident happened. Blaze Face was one of those unusual geldings seen now and then in the West that, as the cowboys expressed it, "liked the little fellers."

The wind and rain at times drove down so hard that the horses jerked up their heads and jostled each other about, each trying for a better place, but it was no use. They had to take the full force of cold rain as it drove against them. At times Cinchfoot could hardly breathe as the rain drove into his eyes and nostrils and even his mouth, but he only stood closer to Blaze Face and snorted to get the water out of his nose. Now and then he would shake his head and stamp the ground in his impatience. The other horses crowded close to Blaze Face and stood with their tails toward the storm, their heads held low. Cinchfoot stood between Blaze Face and another big horse, so that he was a little protected.

The small herd of horses that stood in the driving storm on this day were range horses and therefore they were used to saddles on their backs and cowboys in the saddles. But there were two unusual horses among them. The big black gelding with the white face, known as Blaze Face, didn't like to have anybody on his back. He wanted to run wild and be free, and at the same time take a small herd of other range horses with him. So every spring he got a number of horses that didn't like tame life to run off with him and, as the cowboys said, "look for new country." But he would no more than get his new grazing place picked out than the cowboys would come riding along and drive him and the others back to the ranch for the spring work. Blaze Face, at this time, was seven years old. He seemed to like the yearling colt that stood beside him here in this storm more than any of the "little fellers" he had ever known.

The other unusual horse was this colt, Cinchfoot. Blaze Face stood right beside him and twice, in the driving rain, put his nose on the trembling colt as if he were trying to say, in cowboy language, "Don't be too much troubled, little feller, because I aim to take care of you and we'll get out of all this by and by."

The cattlemen and the cowboys over a wide range knew Blaze Face. He was a cow horse and one of the worst buckers that anyone had ever put a saddle on. But as one of the cow· boys said, he was "plumb crazy about a little colt, him wanting to be more to it than the colt's mammy." And so Cinchfoot had a powerful friend in Blaze Face on this day when it seemed that the rain was surely trying to drown him. Cinchfoot did not know that his life had started out in an unusual way, because he had been born in the summer instead of the spring. He did know that he had about frozen during his first winter and that the

world was certainly a place where he had had
to fight to live almost from the start. But now
that he had lived through the first winter he
felt as though "he was all horse." He knew
what it was to fight generally. So, while he'd
never been in a thing like this before, he went
right on fighting as he had against so many
other things, including cold and the deep
snow drifts of winter. He snorted often as the
rain drove down and, now and then, he tried
to get his head away from the driving sheets
of rain by putting his nose down between
Blaze Face and another horse, but when he
did that, it seemed that a small river ran down
into his nose and tried to strangle him. So he
raised his head a little and took the same posi-
tion as the older horses did and he snorted
and blew the water out of his nose and didn't
try to see, just shut his eyes as they did.

Now it happened that old Blaze Face and
the small herd of range horses were not quite
alone at this time. Two humans were only a
little way off. Two cattlemen, Clem Brown,
the owner of the ranch, and Sam Blades had

been out looking for Blaze Face and the other horses when they saw the storm coming. Clem and Sam, knowing the range, had spurred hard to a shelter they knew about and got into it with their horses. This was an old abandoned mine hole in the hillside just above the plain where the horses now stood. Clem and Sam had taken their horses back into the mine hole, and now both riders stood inside the shelter and looked out at the storm, while the wind drove a fine spray of rain in upon them.

Suddenly, during a flash of lightning, Clem said, "Looky down there, Sam! There's the range horses and Blaze Face!" Sam saw them and the two riders waited for another flash of lightning. After that first flash everything was black darkness, but when the lightning flared again, Clem and Sam saw the horses huddled together, and this time they saw the colt standing with the others. "A colt, and ain't he a beauty!" Clem said, and all at once the small herd of horses below seemed very interesting to the two cowboys.

After a little time, as was usual with these

storms of the West, the rain ceased. It didn't quit by degrees—it stopped as suddenly as it had begun and soon the clouds began to roll away and the sky was as clear as if nothing had happened. The western sun shone fine and beautiful on the drenched earth, and it shone bright and warm on the shivering horses below.

Already Cinchfoot was walking around the herd and he was snorting—snorting and looking at the water tearing along in the stream not far away. He put his nose down to the ground, raised his head and stamped his foot on the wet ground. It was as if he were thinking, "Well! I can't figure all this out, but somebody must be trying to be funny or something! I got about enough of *this*."

But about this time Blaze Face walked up to Cinchfoot and these two nosed each other and seemed to be talking about the matter in their own language, for they made sounds to each other. Blaze Face looked around and snorted as if he might have told Cinchfoot that he, too, didn't care to have much more of this sort of thing. And then, for the first time, Blaze Face, always alert, saw on the hillside a little distance up the slope, the two riders.

Clem and Sam had tried to be quick about it. They had already led their horses to the edge of the mine hole and were just ready to mount and try to "fog" the range horses home. They knew Blaze Face would try to run away. They would just let him go for they knew that, as Clem said, "We always have to run him in alone."

The instant Blaze Face saw the men he began to prance in a small circle, his eyes wide, his tail high. Sam grinned. He said, "Look at Blaze Face! Look at his tail! Did you ever see a horse that could hold his tail as high as he can?"

"No," said Clem, "no other horse could hold his tail that high." And that's all the time there was for words.

Down the rocky hillside Clem and Sam rode. They got into action so quickly they were on their way when Blaze Face shot out for open country. Here a queer thing happened. Clem and Sam spurred hard to get close and swing their loops over Cinchfoot. They figured they would have a pretty hard time driving him in with the other range horses. They knew colts his age that had never seen humans might run clear away.

But just at this time some help was seen not far off. This was three cowboys who had been caught in the storm and who now rode up on a ridge a little to the west of where Clem and Sam happened to be. When the three cowboys looked out and saw the herd of range horses, and at the same time Clem and Sam, they understood everything. But Blaze Face knew what to do, for he had now seen all the cowboys. With a loud snort Blaze Face started to run. The other horses followed him. Blaze Face kept well ahead of all the horses, but Cinchfoot kept right behind him and sometimes he was neck and neck with him. Probably Cinchfoot thought he would get away. Certainly he had, as the cowboys said, "uncorked an awful lot of speed, him being plumb determined to travel to new country."

But Cinchfoot had not yet learned the ways of cowboys. He did not know that no matter how he figured things out, they had a way of doing a better job of figuring than he did. And another thing Cinchfoot did not know was that while all five of the cowboys began to crowd in on each side and behind, they were all looking at him and admiring him. Cinchfoot heard loud yells coming from these humans but he did not know they were saying:

"Whoopee! There's a yearling colt!"

"Daggone his little hide!"

"Yes, how did he ever live through the winter?"

"Why, he's tough as a pine knot, that's how!"

"Certainly! And he don't aim to be caught, not by considerable."

And while the cowboys yelled, their faces were wide with admiring grins for the racing "little feller." But they had no notion of letting him get away. On the contrary; his speed and his jet black coat and silver mane and tail, which now showed plainly, made it the more certain that Cinchfoot would have to go right along with Blaze Face and the other range horses to the big corrals at the ranch house.

Several times, while the race was on, Cinchfoot whirled and tried to run off to one side. It seemed to him that the thing to do was to go the way he wanted, but each time there was a cowboy on a running horse on that side to keep him with the others. And now, on his first meeting with humans, Cinchfoot showed them that his opinion was not the same as theirs. Cinchfoot wanted to stay free always! So did Blaze Face, and somehow on this day he was more determined than ever. He and Cinchfoot ran neck and neck and it was plain these two didn't care where the other horses went; they would go off in *another* direction. All of a sudden Blaze Face saw his chance and he shot out on some level ground toward the west and Cinchfoot followed right beside him. Two cowboys spurred as hard as they could to head them off, but it was no use. They ran like the wind and got away. It seemed that Blaze Face had decided that since he had Cinchfoot for company he was going to take him away and stay away if his legs had anything to do with the matter.

Clem and his cowboys wisely let them go and drove the other range horses on and finally got them where they belonged, in a big corral at the ranch. After the snorting horses were in the corral and the gate was shut the talk was all about the new colt and Blaze Face. It was plain that Cinchfoot no longer needed a mother. Clem said, "He feels plumb growed up, having Blaze Face to teach him, but we'll 'fog' 'em in here tomorrow."

In the meantime Cinchfoot was, for the time, proud of himself. Night had come and the stars were shining out in the Buffalo Springs country where Blaze Face had led him. There was plenty of water and grass here, and after Blaze Face had stopped from his running he nosed Cinchfoot, as he had done since the first week Cinchfoot had been born. They were both hot and sweating, but

they did not care about that. They were free
and that's all that mattered to them.

Blaze Face had tried, during all his seven
years of life, to escape the spring roundup.
And every spring he hated more than before
to have a saddle and a man on his back. Once
he had run miles away and thought he'd never
come back to the range horses. He got away
that spring and met some of the wild horses,
but as Clem Brown said, "a big wild stallion
there almost chewed Blaze Face up." After
he had gotten free he believed he had better
hang around on the outskirts of the range and
get such company as he could among the tame
horses. He liked the company of these range
horses, but he wanted them to stay away from
the place where they had to be in the hands of
the cowboys all summer. And he was so hard
to catch one season that he managed to keep
away until late June. Then Clem and his cowboys surprised him one day, roped him and
brought him in. When they saddled him up
he bucked like a wild cat, but it was no use.
There were too many good riders. Sam

Blades, who rode him that summer, bragged about him: "He's the hardest bucker I ever got up on but he's the best horse, too, him being that full of disgust, he don't get tired at all."

As to Cinchfoot, although he was hardly a year old, Blaze Face knew him pretty well already. Blaze Face could tell that Cinchfoot also had a fighting spirit and he was going to try to stay a long way off from the cowboys if he could. And while Cinchfoot did not know it yet, on this day he proved to the cowboys who chased him that he had two things above the average colt. He had great speed and great determination to go on his own. He wanted to be free, to get clear away from men and stay away. There was one just born that way now and then, and the cowboys liked this kind more than any other. They made the best cow horses if they could be caught. So at this time, Blaze Face and Cinchfoot had one thing in mind. They would watch out for the men and when it got light they would be ready to run again.

After Cinchfoot had eaten grass for some time he felt pretty well. The grass tasted sweet and good. Several times he went over to the springs here and drank beside Blaze Face. The sweat dried on his coat. Now and then, as the two of them bit off the green grass on the level valley, Blaze Face would raise his head and listen. At these times he would hear such sounds as a coyote yipping or maybe an owl hooting in the shadows of a pine woods north of them. Cinchfoot would toss his head up, too, and look in the direction Blaze Face did, but after a little, Blaze Face would put his nose on Cinchfoot's and make some sounds as if he said, "It's nothing—just sounds, nothing more. We can go right on eating and being comfortable." And the two would go on biting off the grass.

Cinchfoot had forgotten about the cowboys. But Blaze Face hadn't. He knew them. More would be seen of them. It would only be a question of when they would be seen. And under the starlight Blaze Face now and then raised his head and looked toward the ridges.

II: *Blaze Face*

IT was almost noon the next day when Blaze
Face and Cinchfoot stood together and
peeped through some tall bushes at the cowboys down on the flats chasing a herd of range
horses toward the distant ranch. The cunning
old Blaze Face, in some way that only animals
understand, had taught Cinchfoot how to hide
and keep still. Blaze Face would have run off
at the first sight of the men on this day, but it
happened that they appeared on the south and
there were so many of them it looked as if he
and Cinchfoot, if they showed themselves,
would have to run north toward the ranch.
Blaze Face had hidden in the brush more
than once and so gotten away. He and Cinchfoot would do that again today; at least that
was what Blaze Face thought. He and Cinchfoot stood close beside each other with their
heads facing the running horses below them.

30

The small herd of range horses that the cowboys were chasing, in an effort to turn them, were average range horses. They would fight for a time to get away but after a while they would give up and turn back the way the cowboys wanted them to go.

While Blaze Face and Cinchfoot remained hidden in the bushes, Cinchfoot got pretty nervous. And once he wanted to run out and away—that was when some of the horses started in his direction—but old Blaze Face stayed quiet and Cinchfoot understood he should do the same. But there was one cowboy in particular who knew the ways of old Blaze Face. That cowboy was Clem. More than once in the spring roundups he had found Blaze Face hiding from him in the brush. Clem was certain that he was doing that now and likely he had the black yearling colt with him. But this was something that Blaze Face didn't know. He thought he could get away by hiding or else he could tell pretty quickly when to run if that time should come.

The cowboys were all well mounted and

feeling good. Loud yells could be heard along with the running and whirling and chasing of the horses. After much running and yelling on the flats below, the herd of range horses were headed toward the distant ranch and a dozen cowboys galloped behind in a trail of dust. But some of the cowboys turned their horses and rode west, as it happened, toward the hiding place of Blaze Face and his small crony. Three of these riders were Clem Brown, Charley Steel and Sam Blades. They were hunting for Blaze Face and Cinchfoot. Clem said, "Blaze Face has got that colt somewhere in the brush and he's hiding with him." And a little later the keen-eyed Clem said, "Wait!" He pulled on the reins, stopping his horse. "Look at them bushes up on the ridge there—see anything?"

All the cowboys grinned. Thinly veiled behind the bushes stood Blaze Face and Cinchfoot. The cowboys did not act as if they saw the two hiding behind the bushes. They knew Blaze Face and they turned as if they were not thinking much about anything and started their horses at a trot toward rolling ground where they wouldn't be seen. They wanted to ride around and so get behind Blaze Face and Cinchfoot, then drive them in toward the ranch. If Blaze Face had been alone they would have let him go until some other time. Clem was grinning as he thought of the wily Blaze Face. During one summer previous Clem had found him, as usual, one of the best of cow horses. He would buck each morning when saddled up and he would often buck when he was nearly home at night.

As the three cowboys rode along together Clem said, "I've rode that Blaze Face now for several summers and he sure hates saddles and straps and buckles, and seems like he hates 'em worse all the time. He bucks whenever he thinks about it. Sometimes he'll be going along on the range and a feller will be sitting on him, half asleep, then all of a sudden the fireworks will start and Blaze Face will go to bucking as if he was saying, 'Why, I'll be daggoned! Now look at me! I been going along here all day and doing all that

feller on my back wanted, and I ain't bucked
a lick! Well, I'll make up for lost time *now!*
Careless of me actually to forget to buck. I'm
almost ashamed to think I'd forget about that
part of it!' "

The fact was Blaze Face had generally gotten away a month earlier every season. Clem
would say, "I'll get him next spring and he'll
have plenty work to do." But the cowboys
here on this day would not let Blaze Face go.
They wanted him and the colt too. Clem did
not let his range colts run out on the wild
range in the winter as some ranchmen did. He
valued his saddle stock and he kept the colts
and mares at the ranch and fed them on rough
feed until spring. In this way he saved many
colts from being pulled down by gray wolves,
and Clem's colts looked well in the spring.

After riding as near as they dared to the
cunning Blaze Face and the little colt the
cowboys scattered and rode a little apart as
they came up. Sudden Blaze Face shot out
with a speed well known to every rider now
after him. Nevertheless, at the end of an hour,

Blaze Face was headed in a course toward the ranch. But try as they would neither Clem nor any of his friends could head Cinchfoot back, although they did not suppose it possible that the colt could run clear away from them all. And when they finally turned Blaze Face and got him going in the right direction, Clem yelled for the riders to let the colt go. He shouted, "He'll foller Blaze Face in anyway!"

After they had galloped on behind Blaze Face for some time they topped a ridge and Clem Brown pulled up his horse to look back. He grinned and yelled to the others, "He's coming! He's lonesome without Blaze Face!"

And it was so. Cinchfoot was trying to see what was being done with Blaze Face, but he did not expect to be caught himself. Even the sight of the men about scared him stiff. It was not so much that he was afraid of being hurt by them. He had had no experience to tell him about that. But he just naturally wanted to be free. While Cinchfoot did not know it, Blaze Face had always been that kind of

horse too. The big difference between Blaze
Face and Cinchfoot was that Cinchfoot had
been given a greater speed than the older
horse. And on this day when Blaze Face
found that he at last had a horse, even if not a
big one, who would try to stay with him out
on the wild range, he had done all he could
not to be turned back. But Blaze Face
couldn't outrun all these cowboys. He had
done his level best and they had got him anyway.

As he ran on now, knowing well that he
would be caught and tied up again, he was
thinking about his small pal somewhere in the
distance behind him, and even though Blaze
Face was breathing hard he would now and
then let out a wild, shrill nicker as he ran.
Then it was that Clem and the others began to
hear another wild, shrill nicker far in the
rear. It was a sound every cowboys knows, no
matter where he hears it—the strange, piercing nicker of a colt. There is nothing else like
it. At the time Clem and Sam and Charley
were riding close together. Clem turned in his

saddle and looked back across a wide level plain stretching miles behind them. He said, "Daggone his little hide, he's coming, coming hard too, but not too hard. He wants to see what we're going to do with old Blaze Face, and Blaze Face sure wants to get to that colt."

Sam said, "Clem, we ain't going to get that colt easy. If anybody thinks he'll come tearing up to the corral after we get Blaze Face in, why they'll be plumb mistaken."

"It's so," said Clem. "That colt ain't going to run up and say, 'Put a halter on me, fellers, I'm plumb itching to be tied up!' We'll get him by deceiving him. And it won't hurt him any. We'll get old Blaze Face into one of the small corrals and we'll tie him in there alone. Then we'll leave the gate open and when it gets dark I'll hide and watch. Some time in the night, if I don't miss my guess, that colt will come up and him and Blaze Face will talk to each other and then the little feller will just have to go in at that gate to see Blaze Face and then I'll slam the gate shut

and we'll have him. I can see now that he's
the kind that will feel like he's being stuck
with pins every time a hand touches him."

"It's so," Charley said. "I can hardly wait
to put my hands on him and feel him quiver
and flinch like he thought a feller was going
to bite him maybe. That's the kind that makes
awful good cow horses."

"*When* you get him!" said Sam. "Only we
ain't *got* him yet!"

It was late when Blaze Face was at last
driven into the small corral. Clem walked in
and tossed his loop over the horse, but Blaze
Face didn't fight when he felt that loop on his
neck. He was too smart to fight a rope for he
had had too much experience. He was watching and he was looking back in the direction
where he had heard Cinchfoot. But there was
no sound back there now and no sign of a
colt.

Blaze Face was tied in a small corral, on
the side farthest from the gate, and the gate
was left open. The sun had gone down by this
time and already the darkness was coming on.

III: *A Waiting Game*

CINCHFOOT couldn't understand why Blaze Face had been taken away from him. Everything seemed wrong after that. Cinchfoot stood on a high hill on the trail over which they had taken Blaze Face. It was dark now and the moon had come up over a long line of hills toward the east. The stars were shining, too, and the western night was about as bright as a night could be. Cinchfoot had already learned that the night had for him both advantages and disadvantages. He knew he could get around and go places in the dark without so much danger of being seen, but at the same time he knew that other things could hide and see *him* and so he might be in danger without knowing where the danger was. That's why Cinchfoot stood on the hill in the silence and looked and waited.

At last he started walking down the hill

and when he was on the level below he started at a gallop across the plain. During the last of the daylight he had seen the place where they stopped with Blaze Face. But it was so far in the distance things looked dim there. He had seen the cowboys on their horses riding around the place and he had seen what he knew was a small herd of horses without men on their backs, horses that were loose but not free! Cinchfoot knew that when those men got up close to a small herd of loose horses they took the horses away with them. He was almost afraid at this time even to think about it. He stopped and stood still for a minute in the moonlight. The wind was blowing in his face and he not only scented the horses but he got the man scent, too. And now he saw a light in the distance. Two of them, in fact. The lights came from two small windows in the ranch house. Cinchfoot snorted a little. After a time he started at a trot. It was night now, so he would come closer to the place. Presently he stopped, listened, snorted and then trotted forward, when he stopped again. This time he got a scent that he recognized. It was that of his pal, Blaze Face. Cinchfoot sent forth a nicker toward his crony. Immediately the nicker was answered by one from Blaze Face.

Cinchfoot went at a gallop now and he didn't stop until he was close enough to the horse corrals to see the horses in one of them, but as yet he couldn't see Blaze Face. Just then a low nicker from Blaze Face told Cinchfoot in what corral he was. And again Blaze Face nickered low to him as if saying, "Come over here, pal! I'm over here." But Cinchfoot was suspicious of things generally around the place. He wanted to be careful. He had not as yet felt the hands of men on him, and while he was looking, he was also ready to run. He was well aware that if the men got him they would hold him so he couldn't get away. He would be like the other horses in the corral, horses that he could now see milling around in there a little way beyond him. The horses did not seem to like it in the corral. Now and then one of them would squeal and Cinchfoot knew what that

sound meant. It meant that the horses in the
corral were quarreling and now and then biting one another. He took a few steps closer to
this corral where the horses were. They again
started milling and squealing and biting.
Once a number of them ran and crowded
against the side of the high pole corral and if
it had not been very strong the horses would
have crashed out. Cinchfoot thought in his
own language, "Yes, they all want to get out
of that place but they can't. These two-legged
animals that ride horses have shut these horses
in here; at least they have had something to do
with it and I'm suspicious. I'll walk around
here and look things over, but I'll take no
chances. I don't aim to let them shut *me* up!
Not by a good deal. I've got plenty things to
do of my own. I'll see now what's the matter
with Blaze Face. It seems he keeps standing
in another place. Ah! there he is, in there, and
the gate open! Yes, there it is, wide open! I'll
nicker to him and see what he says."

Cinchfoot nickered low and Blaze Face
nickered low in return and called Cinchfoot,

telling him to come closer. There was no
doubt about Blaze Face's sincerity, but unfor-
tunately he didn't know what he was calling
Cinchfoot into. Cinchfoot walked up to the
open gate, got scared, snorted, ran off a little
and then back he came. He did this three
times. The third time he galloped up to the
open corral as if this time he surely would go
in and up to Blaze Face, but again he stopped
short, spraddled his front legs to stop himself,
and with his head low, his eyes looking
scared, he snorted again. Somehow that opening seemed suspicious. It looked almost too
easy to go in there. And why wouldn't Blaze
Face come on out? In the same way, why did
the horses in the big corral keep milling
around and squealing and biting each other?
Always before Cinchfoot had seen these same
horses run away from the men even when the
men were a long distance off. But now they
were caught! And so Cinchfoot was suspicious. He wanted so much to run up to his old
pal, Blaze Face. In fact, at times he could
hardly resist. The only way he kept from

going in was to stop suddenly at the opening, whirl and run as hard as he could out on the open plain. He would tear out as if maybe he was going into new country and stay there, but each time he would stop, hold his head high and look back. Then he would hear Blaze Face nicker and back Cinchfoot would come!

It was hard to know which way to run, away from the horse corral or back to it. Then he seemed decided on a plan, and he carried it out. He galloped clear around both the horse corrals, snorting as he galloped as if to scare away anything that was not friendly to him. But Cinchfoot did not happen to dash suddenly into one of the dark stables nearby. If he had he would have startled a cowboy and embarrassed him considerably. That cowboy was Clem Brown. Clem had taken up his place in the dark stall of a stable and he knew he would stay there until morning and watch, unless Cinchfoot at last galloped into the corral and up to Blaze Face. Clem knew that if he could capture the colt this would save a

hard run after him. He knew that if Cinchfoot once dashed into the corral and he could
slip out and shut that gate quick enough, the
colt was his. Clem had taken this dark place
to watch because it was easy for him to see
Cinchfoot and all he did in the bright moonlight outside. At present Clem began to fear
that Cinchfoot would find him! Cinchfoot did
run around another nearby stable. He even
looked in at the door and snorted but there
was nothing inside. He stood there for a minute in the moonlight and Clem could see his
ears moving quickly back and forth. But
Cinchfoot quit his investigation after that and
Clem thought, maybe the reason he didn't run
around and look in at this stall in the stable
was because this building was on a creek bank
and the door here was pretty close to a deep
ravine. Cinchfoot likely did not care to take
any chances there, not knowing much about
the place anyway. So he looked around generally except the one place where Clem was
hiding.

The horses in the big corral all at once got

quiet. They had quit milling around and squealing and biting, for the time at least. Cinchfoot walked up close to this corral and looked in at the horses standing there. As it happened he looked right in the face of an old brown mare that wasn't any too well satisfied at being cooped up in the corral. She snorted loudly when Cinchfoot woke her up, from a dream maybe, and she seemed to say to him, "What do *you* want around here! Waking a person up like that! They'll get *you* next. You better use your legs while you can!" Something like that must have been in what the old mare snorted, for Cinchfoot lit out from the place at a dead run. This time he ran all the way up to the top of a ridge a quarter of a mile away. There in the moonlight he ran back and forth, while he snorted to his heart's content. He was free and he felt good about it. The only trouble out here was he had no company and in particular old Blaze Face didn't seem to leave the corral.

All was still out here along the ridge and in the valley around the ranch. In fact things

were too still. Cinchfoot couldn't hear anything except his own scared snorts and now
and then the yip, yap of a coyote. But pretty
soon another sound was heard. It was the
nicker of a horse that floated out in the night
from a point near the ranch house. Cinchfoot
recognized it because that was the same nicker
he had heard many times before. It was Blaze
Face calling to Cinchfoot and he knew it. No
use to try to run away from it. Nothing was
right, no matter where, unless Blaze Face was
close by. Cinchfoot again started at a run for
the place where that nicker came from. And
a change had come over him now. He was
still afraid, but not so much; he had got a little used to things around the place. As he ran
up close to the corral this time, he looked over
at the ranch house. It looked safe enough. It
was dark there and not a sound came from it.
Cinchfoot snorted loudly as he looked at the
long low house. But nothing happened. The
house remained as before, very quiet. Then
Cinchfoot, his head high, his tail in the air,
ran once around the house and still nothing

happened. Again he looked at the house and blew loudly through his nostrils as if to say, "Well! If that's all there is around here, nothing but the dark, I'll take more chances."

It was while he was in this frame of mind that a new scent came to the nose of Cinchfoot. It was the horse scent but it was not that in either of the corrals. The wind had veered around and now blew across a small creek, with its fringe of woods, a little below the house. Cinchfoot started out to see what was there. He made his way beyond the ranch house and, ready to jump at his own shadow, walked down some shelving ground and up to another corral near the woods by the stream. Cinchfoot at once looked into the corral. Loud snorts from inside greeted him and he saw not only big horses in here but also several colts about the same size as he was. A short time before, these colts had been driven in with some horses and branded. They would be held there a few days and then turned loose again, but they couldn't tell Cinchfoot what had happened to them. He looked at the colts for a brief time, then it seemed to him that he had better find Blaze Face to associate with or he would be left alone permanently. He turned from this place and again trotted close to the ranch house, stopped and snorted. The place was as dark and still as ever. No sign of life there. And while he knew someone was in that place, yet they seemed to be so quiet that he began to lose more of his fear. Again he heard the nicker of Blaze Face calling him and telling him to come up.

Cinchfoot ran to the open gate and again he looked at Blaze Face. At last most of the fear was gone. The space left by the open gate was so wide it seemed one could run out again if things happened. Cinchfoot did not hesitate this time. He leaped forward and in a few jumps he was up to Blaze Face and the two of them began talking to each other with many sounds that both of them understood. Then something happened, and it happened quickly. The corral gate went shut. And at the same time a man was seen outside in the shadows.

Blaze Face lunged back against the rope that held him, and Cinchfoot was so scared he crowded hard against Blaze Face. For a minute the man stood looking in the corral at Cinchfoot, then he walked away from the corral and disappeared in the shadows toward the ranch house.

After some time had gone by Cinchfoot walked over to the gate and investigated it by smelling it. He would smell it for a little, then start back and snort as if the man were still there. And as the night wore on Cinchfoot began to be more and more concerned about getting out. He knew he was caught and all the rest of the night his actions told that he knew. He could not stand long beside Blaze Face. He had to walk around the corral and stop often at the gate to see if there was some way to get out of the place. Now and then he would look toward the ranch house standing so quiet and dark there in the shadows.

As Cinchfoot walked around the corral wondering how he could get out he stopped and looked up at the top poles. They were

about eight feet high. No chance there.
Finally Cinchfoot stopped looking and got
close beside Blaze Face. The two of them
stood in the stillness and as the time passed by
looked mainly toward the ranch house. They
both knew that was where the men were. At
times Cinchfoot heard a noise down in the
corral below, near the creek woods where the
other colts were. They were milling around
down there and he heard the sounds of their
hoofs as they thumped on the hard ground.
After a time the night was almost still. Only
vague sounds could be heard, sounds so vague
no one could tell what made them. And once
a shadow moved silently across the moonlight
when an owl flew over the place and circled
back once to look down in the corral where
Cinchfoot stood. For the time everything
seemed harmless, but Cinchfoot didn't want
to be here knowing he couldn't get out. He
began again to walk around in the corral and
the more he looked at his prison the more
anxious he was to get away. Once he leaped
from the far side of the corral and ran to

Blaze Face and stared at his friend as if to say, "I can't understand this business! We should get out right away. But you seem to want to stay always in the same place. I'm suspicious of the two-legged creatures that I *know* are in that dark building just beyond there. They're mighty quiet *now,* but you know how they are when daylight comes! I have no faith in them. Well, well, this *is* a mess we got into and no way to get out unless maybe we can jump as high as the moon!" And Cinchfoot ran around and around the corral and then back to Blaze Face. He ran so hard and snorted so much he got all the horses on the place scared. They could be heard snorting in the corral down by the creek and in the nearby corral, also. Even some of the saddle horses in the stalls in one of the stables began to snort and it was certain that if Cinchfoot couldn't stand still and sleep he wasn't going to let others sleep either.

After a time he began to realize that the day was coming. At first only the faintest gray streaks began to steal over the place but in a

little time the gray began to show things up
and it was not long until Cinchfoot could see
the ranch house, the trees along the creek, and
the horses in the corral. And now he began to
watch the ranch house. He blew loudly
through his nose, his eyes wide and shining.
He knew where the men were and he knew
that just any time he would see them coming
out of the ranch house and up here to this corral where he and Blaze Face stood. Now and
then he stamped the ground in his fear and
impatience. It seemed, almost, that he
wanted them to come and have it over with.
But Cinchfoot didn't know what was going to
happen to him. All he knew was that he
wanted to be free. He had known this since he
was a little colt. And as the days and weeks of
his short life had gone by he had known it
more and more. It was something fixed in
him. Blaze Face waited as did Cinchfoot at
this time for the coming of the men, but Blaze
Face knew more about what would happen
than Cinchfoot did. Now and then he uttered
a loud, violent snort in answer to that of his

smaller friend, as if to say, "That's right, little feller! Keep it up! It does me good and when they come, fight 'em! Fight 'em and don't quit and some day we'll get out of this and we'll stay in the wild places!"

Suddenly both Cinchfoot and Blaze Face stood very still and looked with blazing eyes at the ranch house. A dozen cowboys were coming out and coming toward the corral.

IV: *Clem Brown*

WHILE Clem and all the cowboys stood around the corral looking in at Cinchfoot, Clem was doing some thinking. After a time he said to Sam Blades, "Sam, I want you fellers to brand him today and be as good to him as you can. I'm awful set on that little horse and I got plans for him. I'm going to brand him and keep him a stallion and I don't want him to see me or smell me so he can associate me with the branding. You fellers go ahead and get that done quick and then we'll let him alone for a week in a corral all by himself. We'll set feed and water in for him and let him alone."

Clem went away and a few minutes later Clem's brand was on Cinchfoot and he was up and tearing around in the corral; and it seemed by the way he looked up at the top poles, he wanted to jump clear over. The

55

brand did not hurt him much. It was more the scare than anything else. It had been done so quickly, and Cinchfoot was so excited, trying to fight, he didn't notice that part of it very much. He felt a little stinging but that was all.

The week went by and the most that Cinchfoot saw of the men was when Clem set water in the corral and plenty of oats. Toward the end of the week Cinchfoot was ready and waiting for the water and oats to be set inside. He had never tasted anything as sweet and good as oats. He would eat all Clem gave him and toward the end of the week when Clem brought the things to him he acted once as if he might come right up and get them, but he stood back and snorted when Clem tried to talk to him.

At the end of the week Clem came out one morning with the cowboys and he was ready to give Cinchfoot a little training. Clem's eyes shone like the eyes of a boy who is glad because he has something fine that he's proud of. He said, "Just look at him, fellers. Now ain't he a beauty! Did you ever see a colt that could beat him? He's horse and all horse and one that's got plenty of fight, too. Look at his mane and tail, not much of a mane and not much of a tail yet, but both of 'em are silver and he's already plumb beautiful. And look at the rest of him! Black as a crow. His kind don't come often. Now look at him run and snort!" Clem's eyes showed how pleased he was with his catch. He opened the gate carefully and with his rope dangling from his hand he came inside the corral and shut the gate. Cinchfoot tore around in a small circle a few times and stopped. He stopped and snorted at Clem who was slowly approaching him. Blaze Face, in a nearby corral, got excited too. He jumped about and snorted, but he had been tied in there with a rope a few feet long so he couldn't tear around too much, and he was careful not to run hard against the rope that held him. Cinchfoot didn't know as yet all that a rope could do. It was about time he should learn, though. And that's what Clem had in mind now as he walked toward

Cinchfoot slowly and quietly. By this time Sam Blades and Charley Steel had come inside and shut the gate behind them. Most of the other cowboys perched themselves on top of the corral.

Up to this time Cinchfoot had not been given a name by any of the cowboys. But he was to be given a name this morning, not only one name in fact, but two of them. The first was given to him by Clem Brown. And Clem gave him this name in the most natural way in the world. The yearling colt, as has been said, was coal black. He had shed his winter coat and there he stood as black as a horse could possibly be, except his silvery mane and tail, which already showed how beautiful both would grow to be in time to come. As Clem walked slowly up to the snorting colt he called out soothingly, "What's wrong, Blackie? You ain't afraid of poor old Clem, are you?" Although Clem Brown was a young man he had a ridiculous way of speaking of himself as "old" to the horses generally. "Come on, Blackie," Clem went on, "I don't aim to hurt you none, only enough to make you a good little horse. How are you this morning?" And then it happened. Clem made a quick motion of his arm and his loop shot out to settle over the head of Cinchfoot. It was the first time he was to know the full power of a rope. It was true he had felt some kind of brief restraint when they had branded him with Clem's brand, but he had been let loose so quickly at the time he didn't find out much about what a rope could do. In fact he had been the most scared when he felt the hands of men on him. There was nothing, as yet, to tell him what a rope could do if he should run against it while it was around his neck. Clem was glad on this morning that the branding of Cinchfoot had already been done for he had in mind to try to make up to the colt when he was once down. Clem knew horses and he knew the things that horses, especially the best ones, like. And he believed Cinchfoot was the kind that, once he understood, would prove to be one of the best.

When the rope settled over his head, Cinch-

foot made a quick jump back, then he rushed
forward and shot past Clem on the dead run.
But Clem was ready. He made a quick half
hitch around a post of the corral and when
Cinchfoot hit the end of the rope he hit it
hard and he went down hard, too. The breath
was almost knocked out of him but he was
going to try to get loose. He was down only a
second, then he jumped up and once more
shot out, and once more he hit the end of the
rope and went down. This time he stayed
down, but not long. Again he jumped up but
he did not run, just stood and looked at Clem
and snorted at him louder than ever. Clem
took the half hitch off the corral post and
again he walked slowly toward Cinchfoot and
talked quietly to him, saying, "You're smarter
than most of 'em. You learn quick. Now, don't
get scared, little feller. I'll give you some nice
brown sugar by and by. You are a real little
horse. They don't come any finer than *you*, but
I don't expect you appreciate such compli-
ments just now!"

Cinchfoot crowded close to the side of the

corral and when Clem got too close he leaped away but stopped before he felt the rope tighten. Already he had learned this part of his lesson. He was still going to get away if he could, but he had learned he must try some way other than running against a rope.

Sam Blades and Charley Steel now watched their chance and in another minute Cinchfoot felt their ropes on his hind legs. He tried to get free, but Charley and Sam had him by all four legs and he was tied down. The thing had been carefully done, and Cinchfoot found, after he was quiet for a few seconds, that he wasn't being hurt. And by the way one man acted now it didn't seem as if things were so bad. This man was Clem Brown.

Clem got down on the ground by Cinch-foot, close to his head, and began talking soothingly to him. At the same time he did a thing unusual among cowboys. Clem took a small cloth sack from his shirt pocket, a sack that held dark brown sugar. He poured some of the sugar in his hand and held it toward

Cinchfoot and said some words that were remembered that day and always afterward,
"Sugar, Blackie! It's good. Eat it!" The other
cowboys were not surprised at Clem doing
this. Ever since they had known him Clem
had done this with his favorite horses. He carried the small sack of brown sugar most of the
time. And Clem, now and then, had had a
horse that would learn to like the sugar so
well he would follow him like a dog, nickering for it. But Clem knew there was no chance
of Cinchfoot getting interested in the sugar at
this time. He only wanted to make a beginning of showing Cinchfoot that he would
have good treatment. When the sugar was
held too close Cinchfoot snorted. But Clem
was patient. Now and then he got his hand on
Cinchfoot's neck and scratched him a little.
This went on for some time and Cinchfoot
began to have a queer feeling. He began to
feel that this human wasn't so much to be
feared. And when the brown sugar was held
pretty close a few more times, Cinchfoot was
not so badly scared but that he could smell it,

But that was all. The smell was as near as Cinchfoot would go at this time. Clem kept on talking to him and getting him to see that at least these human hands that were now rubbing him wouldn't hurt, and saying now and then as he pushed the sugar up close to him, "Sugar, Blackie. It's good. Eat it! Sugar!"

Then Clem got up quiet and easy and said, "Sam, bring in that light saddle!" This was done and the next thing Cinchfoot knew he had that thing cinched on him and he was on his feet with a long rope on his neck. He went into the air so fast that he brought a yell of joy from the cowboys on top of the corral. It looked as if Cinchfoot were saying in their language, "So! You want to see what *I'll* do with this contraption, do you? Well, I'll *show* you what *I'll* do! I'll buck it into the next county—that's exactly what I'll do!" Clem grinned happily. He said, "He's going to make an awful fine stallion and by the way he bucks now I don't reckon any feller will be able to set up in the middle of him, except me!"

After some time of the wildest leaping and bucking, Cinchfoot did an unusual thing, the thing that gave him the name we have been calling him. He flopped down on the ground on his side, put his head down on the ground also, and began to try with all his might to get his hind hoof against the cinch of the saddle and paw it off! For a second the cowboys did not know what was going on but after a few attempts by Cinchfoot they could see. Of course he could not reach the saddle cinch with his hoof, yet he certainly tried hard to do so. But being a horse, and coupled up the way he was, he could do nothing more than try to reach the cinch with a hind foot. Up he jumped, again and again he leaped around the corral making the cowboys there run out of his way, and this time he seemed to buck harder than ever. He paid no attention to Clem or anyone else who was in his way. He seemed to feel he needed all that corral to himself, and the cowboys got out of his way in a hurry and let him have it. He stopped with a final snort and probably would have gone at it again, but he was taken in hand now with the ropes and the saddle was removed.

Cinchfoot looked at all the cowboys as they watched him. He looked and snorted and raised his head and tail and pranced around. Then he looked into the other corral at Blaze Face, and snorted as if to say, "What kind of a party is this, anyhow? Them putting such a rig on me and thinking I'll do nothing—I won't have it!"

It was now that the name of Cinchfoot was first given to him. It was Sam Blades who said, "He's a kind of a little Cinchfooter, him being determined to paw the saddle cinch off with his hind foot!" From this, the name Cinchfooter was shortened to Cinchfoot.

Clem looked at Cinchfoot and said, "He's the kind of little horse that'll foller me around like a dog when I get him to eating brown sugar from my hand."

"Which he won't do," said Sam, "on account of old Blaze Face has got him plumb educated his way already."

During the bucking of Cinchfoot, and even

when he was tied down, Blaze Face had stood in his corral, tied up as he was, but showing as much interest in what was being done to Cinchfoot as Cinchfoot himself. Blaze Face had kept up a loud, wild snorting and jumping around—about all he could do. Once Blaze Face whirled about and taking a good look at the cowboys perched up on top of the corral, he let out a blast from his nostrils that showed how he felt about this business. It was as if he said, "The *idea!* A lot of you two-legged persons jumping onto a little feller like him! Why, him and me hates even to *look* at such as you!"

Clem grinned and said, "Blaze Face is saying to Cinchfoot, 'Don't you mind *them* too much, little feller. One of these times you and me'll get plumb loose from all of 'em and we'll hightail it for new country permanent!' "

Clem looked at Blaze Face then, grinned, and said, "All right, fellers, saddle up Blaze Face. I aim to ride him. Saddle him up and give us plenty of room on account he's plumb unsocial at such times."

All of the cowboys, except Charley and Sam, stayed on top of the corral. Pretty soon Charley and Sam, Sam carrying the saddle, went into the corral where Blaze Face was. He took one look at the saddle and before they got up to him he began to buck and pitch. Sam grinned and said, "He's feeling so plumb obstinate that *this* time maybe he'll throw Clem. It would be awful nice if he would!"

V: *Looking Toward the West*

THE saddle was strapped on Blaze Face and Clem mounted. Now came a battle that the finest riders in the Bar-Z outfit admired. Blaze Face did not take time to bawl as the small bronchos did. He was no broncho, any-way. He was a big horse weighing twelve hundred pounds and he was not only much stronger than the average range horse but was quick as a cat and cunning too. He had more tricks than the ordinary bucking horse. One of these was to jump high, come down on all four feet like the ordinary buckers, but when he landed he'd start whirling as he bucked. Blaze Face had thrown most of the other cowboys of this outfit by this trick but he had never been able to throw Clem. He had watched him buck with another cowboy one day and when he saw the trick, Blaze Face could not throw Clem again. The only way he could be thrown by Blaze Face would be out on the range when Clem forgot the kind of horse he was riding. But Clem wasn't the kind to do this.

Blaze Face on this morning fought hard to buck Clem off. And what was more he was going to keep at it as long as that cowboy was on top of him and as long as Blaze Face had any power left, for that was the kind of battler Blaze Face was.

And while this was going on Cinchfoot stood watching and snorting in another corral. Charley Steel and Sam Blades stood inside the corral near the gate where the battle was going on. The other cowboys, on top of the corral, were yelling their admiration for their chief. "Stay a long time, Clem!" they shouted.

"Look at him buck!" yelled Sam Blades. "He's maybe telling that colt, Cinchfoot, 'Looky here, little feller! Watch how *I* treat 'em! This is the way to do when one of 'em tries to set up on you! *I* aim to give 'em plenty —when the time comes, *you* do the same. Try to throw 'em so hard there won't be enough

left of 'em for a mess! Daggone such creatures as tries to tell *me* what to do. I'll let 'em know I ain't agreed!' "

Three times Clem was almost thrown off balance but he was still riding when Blaze Face quit bucking. And although Blaze Face was puffing, he flashed the whites of his eyes and Clem understood that he would buck again after he was rested. But Clem liked Blaze Face because of his fighting spirit.

"All right, fellers!" Clem called. "Me and Blaze Face is ready now. Let's go! And we got to keep him and that Cinchfoot at the ranch from now on. From this time on we'll keep 'em right here at the ranch, summer and winter. Otherwise Blaze Face will take Cinchfoot and travel away."

Clem and the other cowboys now rode out on the range for the regular work of the day. Clem knew Blaze Face was in trim for the work. He was as hard as iron, a mighty good cow horse, but he had to be watched always. Blaze Face, as has been stated, was the kind that had to be watched *all* the time a cowboy rode him or that cowboy might find himself on the ground and Blaze Face running away, thinking he would stay free.

When Clem started away on Blaze Face there was heard behind him and the other riders a loud, shrill nicker. It was from Cinchfoot. And he not only nickered once but many times, one loud, piercing call after another. Clem and the others knew Cinchfoot was calling for his pal. And then Blaze Face began to nicker back, whirling and jumping wildly.

It was evening when they all rode back, just a little before sundown. But when they were still a good distance away they heard that same wild, piercing nicker again—the call of Cinchfoot for his friend. And as they rode closer they could see Cinchfoot tearing around in the corral. He would run and nicker, and snort and nicker again. Blaze Face began to nicker and he tried to run away from Clem to get to the corral where Cinchfoot was. Clem rode up to the corral and while he was taking the saddle from Blaze

Face he and Cinchfoot kept nickering and talking to each other. When Clem turned Blaze Face into the corral with Cinchfoot they hurried to each other and began to rub each other with their noses and talk excitedly. The cowboys stood looking and grinning. Clem said, "Can you beat it? Them two are certainly awful good cronies. And, come the time they was to get clean loose again out on the range, it would take all the horses on the ranch to ketch 'em."

A week now went by in which Clem and Cinchfoot got to know each other better, and the more Cinchfoot got acquainted with Clem the better he liked him. Every morning Clem would come out to the corral with something in his hand that had the most delicious taste Cinchfoot had ever known. And each time Clem came up he would say, "Sugar, Blackie, sugar! It's good!" And Cinchfoot would eat all there was and then put his nose close to Clem as if he were trying to get some more.

Clem thought now it was time to let Cinchfoot have more space to run around in and so he and Blaze Face were turned loose in a small pasture close by. This pasture was unusually well fenced with five strands of tight barbed wire. But neither Blaze Face nor Cinchfoot would try to run against the fence. They had both learned what a rope would do. And once a range horse learned that lesson he was afraid of a rope, or anything stretched along between posts that even looked like a rope. It had been a rope when they ran against it that had thrown them to the ground, hard. And they remembered. So all that summer they made no effort to break out. They would only stand near the fence at night, after the cowboys had gone to bed, and Blaze Face and Cinchfoot would look out in the distance, with the moon and stars shining overhead, and think how fine it would be if they *could* get out—and sometime, Blaze Face thought, they *would* get out!

By the end of the first month Cinchfoot had come to think a lot of that cowboy, Clem. By that time Cinchfoot would not only eat brown sugar out of Clem's hand and nicker but he'd even beg for Clem to come back when he walked away. Clem would at times go back to the house and get him some more sugar. One morning he did this three times until Sam Blades said, "Clem, he's et too much already. It might give him the stumick-ache or something."

"It's so," said Clem as he scratched Cinchfoot's neck. "I must not give him too much, for I sure wouldn't give this little horse anything that would hurt him."

But the queer thing about it was, Blaze Face would never eat any sugar Clem or anyone else offered him. All they got for their trouble was a wild snort from Blaze Face and he backed as far away as the corral or fence would let him. There he would stand and keep right on snorting as if to say, "Not *me!* I ain't got no confidence in humans—not any!"

At times, when Cinchfoot would come up to Clem and start to lick the sugar from his palm, Blaze Face would snort wildly as if trying to get Cinchfoot to run away. Maybe he was saying, "Don't take anything from 'em, little feller! I don't trust any of 'em. Keep away. It's a trick maybe!" But at such times even the scared snorts of Blaze Face couldn't scare Cinchfoot away from Clem. After he had licked up the sugar he'd even half close his eyes while Clem scratched his neck. By the middle of the summer, when Clem walked out in the morning to the pasture and Cinchfoot saw him, he would nicker and come at a run. And he'd have to plump his legs out in front of him to put on the brakes so he wouldn't run against the gate or Clem. It seemed that Cinchfoot was saying in his nicker, "Well, well! So you *have* come finally! I thought you were a long time about it this morning. I'm about starved for that sweet stuff and I hope you got plenty of it!" At such times Blaze Face would run some distance behind Cinchfoot. He would come running and snorting but always he'd stand a good distance away and snort and prance around to tell Cinchfoot how careless and reckless he was with this cowboy, Clem.

In this way the summer went by.   Cinchfoot didn't live in a very big world during these days. It was only as big as the pasture fence on four sides. But he did a great deal of looking around and exploring while Blaze Face went out on the range to carry Clem around. Cinchfoot would eat grass for a few hours and then he would go all over the place, sniffing at the bunch grass and at times sniffing at a clump of big granite rocks that lay in one corner of the pasture. Sometimes when he would put his nose up to these big rocks he'd jump back and snort and once he had reason to do this. A big rattlesnake was coiled there. It raised its head from its coils but Cinchfoot leaped back to safety. He was very frightened. It happened late in the afternoon and some of the cowboys were riding home, among them Clem. He saw the actions of Cinchfoot near the rocks in the pasture and about that time Cinchfoot saw Clem. With a loud, scared snort Cinchfoot came running toward the pasture gate and when Clem got off his horse and walked inside the pasture Cinchfoot went running back to the pile of rocks. Standing off a safe distance he snorted wildly as if to say to Clem, "Take a look at *that* thing, will you! I don't know what it is but it's certainly nothing to play with! *Look* at it!"

Clem grinned broadly. He picked up a large stone and struck the big rattler and killed it.

"There you are, little feller," Clem said, walking up and putting his arm over Cinchfoot's neck. "You didn't know what it was, but being an awful smart little horse you did know it was plumb dangerous. When you get to be a big horse you'll be the kind that can take care of yourself."

Cinchfoot spent much of his time in the late afternoons standing close to the west side of the pasture fence looking out on the range. He was looking for signs of both Clem and Blaze Face. Sometimes, for more than two hours, he would nicker wildly across the plains for them. And although Blaze Face was no friend to Clem or any other human, still Cinchfoot found both of them friends to him. So he wanted both of them. He wanted Clem because of the brown sugar and because it was pretty fine to have his neck scratched, and he wanted Blaze Face because he was such fine company out here in the pasture.

But Blaze Face never changed. He was the same bucker when Clem saddled him each morning. He wanted the freedom of a vast country and Clem and the others knew it. Often at night when there was no one to see but Cinchfoot, he would walk rapidly around that pasture fence, at the same time looking over it, and in some way he would make Cinchfoot want to go with him. But as soon as Cinchfoot would see Clem coming out in the early morning he would forget he wanted to run away. He thought of nothing at such times but Clem and how good it was to see him.

When the summer had gone by and the fall nights came again, frosty and cold, Cinchfoot was put in a corral close to the horse stables where he could go in at night. And he had plenty to eat. He had oats and hay and he filled himself up so that he kept right on growing through fall and winter. Blaze Face, too,

was kept at the ranch this winter. Clem and
the others had seen for a long time that Blaze
Face wanted to run away to the wild places
and if let loose he might leave for good and
take some range horses with him.

When spring came again and Cinchfoot
had shed his winter coat, he was a beauty. His
coat was a shiny black and his silver mane and
tail were getting long and beautiful. He
seemed to know he was a beauty by the way he
held his head up and, now and then, pranced
around in the smaller pasture. For that was
his home again this second summer. Clem said
what all the cowboys thought one evening
while Cinchfoot was licking brown sugar
from his hand, "Now *ain't* he a purty and
gentle young stallion? Not many as fine-look-
ing as he is and he's gentle, too."

"But wait till you try to get up on him
later!" said Sam Blades.

"Yeah, Clem, wait till that time comes and
then see how gentle he is!" said Charley Steel.

"I'll ride him," Clem grinned. "He couldn't
buck worse than Blaze Face."

The time on the ranch went fast. There was always work to do. Every day of the spring and summer and fall was a hard day. No loafing among the cowboys at such times. Only for a little while in the evening after supper did they have time to talk and tell the happenings of the day. And almost every evening Clem, who rode Blaze Face, had something to tell about what Blaze Face had done. "He was plumb crazy to get clear out from under a feller and go to the wild places and live there," Clem said. "He sure don't like to have fellers strap him all up with rigs and then have someone like me get up in the middle of him and make him pack me around all day. Why, he jumps and shies at nothing at all, just to get me off!" Then Clem grinned pleasantly. "But I don't blame him. If I was him I'd do the same! He's an awful good cow horse."

When the winter passed and spring again came, Clem and his cowboys were glad. This was the time on the range when cowboys and horses took a new interest in life generally. It was fine to see the green leaves on the wil-

lows and cottonwoods along the little streams
and even the pines and cedars seemed to be
greener and more alive than in the cold of
the winter.

Clem and his cowboys felt the new thrill in
the air and they sang as they saddled up their
horses, and many times they would sing when
they rode in at night from the day's work.
They were glad to be alive out here and feel
the horse and saddle under them. Even the
bucking of the horses in the morning at the
start of the day's work was enjoyed.

Cinchfoot now enjoyed things more than
ever. He felt himself getting stronger and
bigger as the days went by. Sometimes it
seemed to him as if he'd have to try to jump
clear over the eight-foot corral that Clem put
him in. But he never tried that and more and
more he liked Clem. He not only liked him
because the brown sugar was still brought
out each morning, but Cinchfoot liked Clem
because he found it was pretty fine just to have
him around. But Cinchfoot still hated the saddle. And no matter how many times Clem put

the saddle on him Cinchfoot would buck as
hard as he could to get it off and then he did
that unusual thing. He would flop down on
his side and try to paw the thing off by trying
to reach the saddle cinch with his foot. But
naturally, he couldn't even touch the cinch.

Clem only grinned at Cinchfoot and said,
"He's a different kind of little horse. He's
plumb obstinate that way and that shows he's
better and smarter than the common run of
horses."

So the summers passed and the winters,
with the cold and snow, until Cinchfoot was
about five years old. Clem had waited that
long before trying to ride him. At last the time
had come for that, Clem thought, and one
morning in the presence of the other cowboys, he put the saddle on Cinchfoot and got
on him, but without spurs or quirt, for Clem
never used such things when he rode a bucker.

Cinchfoot started bucking and Clem found
him the hardest horse to ride he had ever
mounted. Cinchfoot was now big and mighty
strong. He was not like the bronchos that

weighed maybe around eight hundred pounds. He was a magnificent young stallion weighing at least twelve hundred pounds and he was mighty quick in his actions. He bucked so hard and so fast that the other cowboys knew that none but a top rider like Clem could stay there long. But Clem did stay and it looked as if maybe Cinchfoot would have to give up when, all at once, he used a trick that afterward made him famous as a bucking horse. He jumped high in the air, as he had done before, then plunged down on all four legs at once as the ordinary horse might do; but the minute he hit the ground he went up again and swept sidewise—and that was the trick. Clem was thrown on the ground before he knew what had happened. By the quick side motion, as he reared up, Cinchfoot had thrown Clem out of balance. The rest was easy. Clem landed in the dust of the corral and at once got up grinning. Cinchfoot whirled and stood facing him, his eyes wide and seemingly puzzled as if he said, "Well! That's that! Now let's act natural!"

Then an unusual thing happened. Clem said, "Sam, get me some brown sugar!" While Sam hurried to the cook for sugar the cowboys yelled, "Why, Clem, he won't eat sugar *now!* He's too het up and excited."

But when Clem got the sugar in his hand, he said, "Of course he'll eat it." He held out his hand toward Cinchfoot and said, "Sugar, Blackie. Come and get it!" For a few seconds Cinchfoot stood and looked at Clem but as the voice kept calling he took a long breath as if he were a little rested and then walked straight up to Clem and began to lick the sugar from the palm of his hand.

Charley said, "Clem, nobody could be such a granny to a horse as you and looks like he'd forgot already about you trying to set up on him. But I guess he's too tough to be rode. Who do you want to try him next?"

"Me," Clem said. "I know how to stay on him, now!"

After Cinchfoot had eaten sugar and seemed calm again, Clem scratched his neck for a minute and then he was in the saddle.

"Whoopee!" yelled the cowboys and again Clem did his best and this time after many minutes Clem's best was good enough. He stayed. He stayed when Cinchfoot tried that clever trick, although Clem was almost thrown, and twice again Cinchfoot tried the trick but Clem was ready. When Clem got off he knew that here was a horse that very few riders could stay on. That one trick would take care of them and it wasn't every rider that would see how it was done. Clem patted his horse and scratched his neck and once more after some coaxing Cinchfoot lapped up some brown sugar.

Clem didn't say anything about how hard he found it to stay on Cinchfoot. He waited until the next day and let the other riders try to ride him. Sam Blades and Charley Steel were thrown in short order. And when Cinchfoot threw several more riders the saddle was taken off. While little was said, the cowboys were all proud of Clem. He was a top rider of the top riders. They knew it.

That night in the ranch house Sam said,

"Clem, these rodeos is beginning to start up over the country. Cinchfoot would give fellers at a rodeo plenty of bucking."

The talk then was along this line and one of the riders who had seen a rodeo told how the horses were handled.

In the meantime Cinchfoot and Blaze Face were out in the pasture standing very close together, looking out on the shadowy plain that stretched away into the west. And on this night, as other nights, something seemed to be calling them, always calling them to the far places.

VI: *Felipe and Carlos*

IT happened one night during this spring when Cinchfoot was five years old. He and Blaze Face were together, as usual, in the pasture not far from the ranch house. Clem and all the cowboys were sound asleep in their beds.

Up to this time Cinchfoot had not been far from the ranch. The only time he ever saw the country beyond was when Clem put the saddle on him and rode him about ten miles out on the range. Usually Clem did not ride him that far. Cinchfoot, after the first few times Clem got on his back, did not buck. That is, he didn't buck when Clem got on him but was as wild as ever when Sam or Charley or any of the others tried to ride him, although they did not hurt him in the least. And Cinchfoot, all this time during the summer nights out here with Blaze Face, had wanted to get out and go far in the distance where something seemed to call him. He had been that way from the time he was a little colt when Blaze Face began to take care of him. Clem had seen many times how Cinchfoot ran around and nickered when he saw Blaze Face coming home at night and he was sure that if Blaze Face got away he would take Cinchfoot with him. While the friendship between these two was unusual, now and then experienced cattlemen in the West had seen an attachment between two strong horses such as Cinchfoot and Blaze Face.

It happened that, even before this spring, there had been many drifting cowboys who had stopped at the ranch and Cinchfoot was already known far and wide for his strength and beauty. It was known, too, that Clem Brown was the only cowboy who could ride Cinchfoot, that Cinchfoot would no longer buck with Clem, and that his trick of bucking and suddenly swerving to one side as he went up unseated the best of riders. Clem had been offered fancy prices for him but he turned them all down and was decided all the more not to part with Cinchfoot.

But on this spring night, when the grass was growing everywhere on the range, Cinchfoot and Blaze Face got away. In some way the wire loop at the top of the wire gate of the small pasture was not down far enough on the post and in the night, while Blaze Face was rubbing his nose on the post, he somehow pushed the wire loop up and the whole gate fell down. Blaze Face snorted in surprise at the sudden movement of the gate and so did Cinchfoot who was standing near. But the next thing that happened was that Blaze Face walked out and Cinchfoot walked out close behind. Cinchfoot had always followed the lead of Blaze Face and he did that now. When Blaze Face started to run Cinchfoot ran alongside and both of them kept right on running. They were both thrilled with this thing of being free and the farther they ran the more thrilled they were and the more they wanted to remain free.

Clem was the first one next morning to find

that the gate to the pasture fence was open and that Blaze Face and Cinchfoot had gone. But Clem was a practical ranchman. He didn't waste any time complaining about it. He set to work with the other cowboys to try to catch up with Blaze Face and Cinchfoot and run them back to the ranch. For three weeks this was tried. On two occasions a dozen or more mounted cowboys saw the horses and tried to run them back, but Blaze Face and Cinchfoot outran them all. It was seen that Blaze Face had a peculiar influence on Cinchfoot now. He seemed as wild as Blaze Face and it was plain, too, that when it was a question of running Cinchfoot was the swifter of the two.

One evening after the second race had failed, Clem said to the other riders, "It's no use. We can't get 'em that way. We'll have to get Blaze Face by some kind of trick; then Cinchfoot, I think, will come back to be with him."

Several days went by after this and nothing happened. Clem kept hoping that some night when he rode home he would see Cinchfoot there by the pasture fence—"Waiting for some sugar, maybe."

But nothing came of it. Cinchfoot was having the time of his life running wild and free.

While this was going on there were two men who had heard about the horses getting away. These two men were more cunning and deceitful than most of the cowboys farther to the north. And it happened that one night these two were riding toward the region where, they had heard, Blaze Face and Cinchfoot were running free. A light wind was blowing across the rolling plain as the two men rode on through the night toward the northwest.

The two riders were Felipe and Carlos, Mexican cowboys, both young men and excellent in their work of outwitting and capturing horses. These two had worked mainly in the Southwest and any number of men on the vast ranches there would say without hesitation that the two Mexican riders were the most clever and cunning with a rope they had ever seen. Either Felipe or Carlos could throw their rope over any foot of a cow or a horse they wished and sometimes, to show their skill, they did the same thing with a calf, and that was no easy matter. But both Felipe and Carlos had something in them besides skill as cowboys. And this was a strange cunning. It was this cunning that led them on through the silent starlit night at this time.

Felipe and Carlos were riding north for a definite purpose because the fame of a great black stallion with silver mane and tail had reached them. In fact the fame of this great horse was known by cattlemen over quite a wide territory. Various tales had been told about his beauty and speed and that he was quite wild. One night in New Mexico, Felipe and Carlos had talked until nearly morning with two riders from the north who had seen Cinchfoot at a distance and told of his great beauty and speed.

The two cowboys had told Felipe and Carlos that the great stallion, Cinchfoot, had broken away from the restraints of men and that in company with a big black gelding, known as Blaze Face, had taken to the wild, and that the chief occupation of the two seemed to be that of running off the other range horses. Many strange tales were told of the lives of these two who roamed the wild. It was told how the big young stallion and the big gelding, Blaze Face, had formed a strange friendship, and it was told that the friendship had started when the now famous stallion was a small colt.

It was in the days when the rodeo was just coming into its own, and Felipe and Carlos, some time before, had had a long talk with a man who owned a rodeo. He told them that if they could get two or three of the right kind of horses that would buck and never stop, and so furnish some real entertainment, he would pay a fancy price for them.

So it was that Carlos and Felipe, knowing about Blaze Face and Cinchfoot, said that these two would surely do. They would get them and then head into the distant place where the rodeo man would be ready for them and their "buckers." The only thing now necessary was to get these two horses. An impossible job for many but Felipe and Carlos knew how to proceed.

As the two of them rode on through the night they talked low and laughed a little at what they supposed was their fine prospect. The English of Carlos and Felipe was a mixture of many brands of English as they had heard it from Americans who had come into the Southwest from many parts of the country. And now as they rode along they tried to talk their best English because they knew that presently they would need it. They were already in the region where they wanted to spend a couple of days at some ranch and so get some information about the whereabouts of Cinchfoot and Blaze Face.

At nearly three o'clock in the morning Felipe and Carlos hobbled their horses and lay down for sleep. It was daylight when they awakened. They mounted and rode on, arriving at a ranch at noon. Strangers here, as elsewhere in the West, were given food and lodging and no questions asked.

Felipe and Carlos remained at the ranch

two days and in that time, by an occasional question and listening carefully, they learned where to ride. They learned some facts that were very valuable to them for capturing Cinchfoot and Blaze Face. First, they learned that no matter where Blaze Face was, there Cinchfoot would be also. This was known by the cattlemen far and wide. They also learned that Blaze Face wanted just as much to be with Cinchfoot as Cinchfoot wanted to be with him. They also learned that Cinchfoot, in particular, had such speed and endurance that they never could hope to capture him by running after him. In the same way they discovered that Blaze Face was no common range horse that could be run down by a number of well-mounted cowboys, and that Blaze Face always saw them when they were far off. So, cunning must be used. But both Felipe and Carlos had this as a native gift.

They rode forth from the ranch that morning and disappeared in the west as mysteriously as they had come. But nothing was thought of this. Such things were common in those days.

In the meantime Cinchfoot was having the most wonderful time of his life. He ran over the vast country as wild and free as the wildest of wild horses. So did Blaze Face. Sometimes they were so jubilant at their new-found freedom they would nose each other and playfully chew at each other's necks like two puppies. But always they were alert, and always they managed to see any dim shape that showed up on a hill or distant ridge. At the end of their first week of freedom in this distant region they found one morning, to their great joy, several old and rather broken-down range horses that had seen their best days, so that the cowboys in this territory did not trouble to try to round them up and drive them in. Here was more company and it seemed now that perfect days had come. But neither Cinchfoot nor Blaze Face had the least notion that these old, broken-down horses were to lead them into a trap laid by cunning men.

Fortunately for the purpose of Felipe and

Carlos, water was scarce in this wild region. The only drinking place for the horses was a spring at the base of a high, steep hill. The spring murmured its way out under the shadows of a tall lone pine. Around the spring for some distance on the level land grew clumps of brushy thickets, but in front of the spring was an open space of several yards. It was through this open space that the old range horses had, for weeks past, come to drink. And Cinchfoot and Blaze Face, following their lead, had learned to come here for water also. It seemed safe enough to them since the old horses, without hesitation, walked on through the lanes in the brushy thickets and up to the shadows under the tall pine near the tinkling spring.

Not far to the north of the spring lay a little green valley that was ended on the north by a high rocky wall cut down through the hillside. The hill was also steep on the east and west of the spring so that no horse would care to climb it. In this way the horses that fed on the green grass here could not see any distance except toward the south, but the old range horses had entered the place as if all was safe. Here also, this day, came Cinchfoot and Blaze Face. A short distance below the place where the horses were grazing and on the east side, near the hill, was a pine woods. The trees were so close together that the ground was bare except for the pine needles that lay thick everywhere. The whole place at the time seemed quiet. The wind was blowing low from the west. Cinchfoot and Blaze Face were both hungry and they were grazing with the other horses and seemingly at ease except now and then when Blaze Face would raise his head quickly and look about him. But watchful and cunning as Blaze Face was, he was not as cunning as man. Two riders at this time, after long maneuvering, had got into the pine woods and with the wind favorable for them they were peeping through the pine branches toward the horses. The two riders were Felipe and Carlos.

Here they had a whispered consultation. They knew that Cinchfoot and Blaze Face would run in only one direction to escape. That would be straight south. So, if Felipe and Carlos should ride out of the woods and toward the grazing horses, they would try to rush directly past the two riders.

Never before had these Mexican cowboys had a chance to catch such desirable horses. They must make the most of it. They quickly decided they would ride out of the woods at a run and straight toward the grazing horses, and that both would try for the same horse, Blaze Face, since they believed that if they could catch him they could use him to trap Cinchfoot. They believed this from the stories they had heard concerning the strong attachment of these two horses.

Accordingly, when Felipe and Carlos got their coiled ropes ready, they guided their horses carefully to the edge of the woods, then both clapped the spurs to their mounts and they shot out toward the grazing, unsuspecting horses. All the horses threw up their heads. For a tense second Blaze Face and Cinchfoot looked, then the wily old Blaze Face understood everything and he knew he could do but one thing, try to rush past the two oncoming riders. Blaze Face uttered one wild snort and so did Cinchfoot. They tried to make the run side by side but two of the old horses crowded between them and they separated, running on either side of the old horses.

Instantly the two Mexicans saw this and instantly they acted. They rode straight toward Blaze Face. And as this great gelding was almost alongside them, both Felipe and Carlos began to swing their loops. The loop of Carlos shot out. It struck Blaze Face only on the ears as he cleverly ducked and it slid off, but the wily Felipe had been watching for this and even as Blaze Face's head went down and the loop of Carlos slid off, the loop of Felipe dropped over the head of Blaze Face and that experienced horse stopped instantly when he felt the rope tighten on his neck. He was caught and he knew what a rope would do to him, how painful it was to run against it. He stopped, and stood with wide eyes looking at his captors.

Cinchfoot and the other horses ran on still free, but farther down the valley Cinchfoot turned, stopped, with his head high, his eyes blazing, and let out a loud nicker for Blaze Face. But he saw it was no use. Blaze Face could not come. Something had happened to him. He was standing there while the two men were getting off their horses and were walking up to him. That was bad, Cinchfoot knew. Blaze Face was caught. He nickered again and three times he sent forth his wild plaintive call to Blaze Face. Then Cinchfoot became so scared about it all he turned and ran on toward the other horses. To his surprise the old horses had already stopped and all were grazing again. He turned again when he came to the top of a ridge and looked back. In the distance he saw the two riders and he saw his pal, Blaze Face. He was being led by one rider while the other man rode behind him. Cinchfoot snorted, then wheeled and looked at the old horses down in the valley. He could no longer be satisfied with them. He wanted to be with his friend of other days, the one horse who had befriended him, fought other vicious horses away from him and stayed by him day and night, never once running away and leaving him. Cinchfoot would not run away from his friend now. He started at a trot on top of the ridge and moved in a great circle, but always keeping in sight the now captured Blaze Face and the two men who seemed to be doing something with him there. When evening began to settle over the western plains, Cinchfoot was still at a distance, calling to Blaze Face.

"Good!" said Felipe. "Now, Carlos, we do as we say. We fix ropes tonight by spring and tie this Blaze Face close to water and we get that fine black horse with white mane and tail and we have—what they call it?—two beauties!"

So it happened that when the twilight began to fade into the night and the stars peeped down, Blaze Face found himself tied to the pine tree beside the spring. And there were now two loops spread on the ground just a little way from him, ropes with the loops spread

and ready and at the end of these long ropes
hidden in a thicket were Felipe and Carlos.
They had concealed their own horses in the
pine woods to the west. And they had been
careful to find a hiding place for themselves
so that if Cinchfoot and the other horses came
back here to drink, there would be no wind to
tell of Felipe and Carlos. But Cinchfoot did
not know all this. He could only use the wind
to tell him of danger if the wind blew toward
him from the direction in which there was
danger. But the wind at times was treacherous.
There were times when it would not help him.
If he and the others should come along on
their trail to the spring the wind would help
the two men hiding behind a thicket. Felipe
and Carlos were watching, waiting, and as
still as a wild animal who watches and waits
for another approaching animal. An hour
later, the moon pushed up from the eastern
hills and the bare place lay white and silent
around the spring. But the ropes with their
loops cleverly laid could not be seen because
they had been covered with dust. There

seemed to be here only the tinkling spring, inviting horses to drink, and what was unusual, a horse now stood by the spring, just stood and looked out in the moonlight. And that was all he could do, for it was Blaze Face who was tied there.

VII: *Treachery at the Spring*

BLAZE FACE stood, tied as he was to the tree by the spring, and made no sound for some time. He only moved about restlessly and looked as best he could into the shadows, trying to see Cinchfoot out on the plain beyond. But at last he could wait no longer. He sent forth a loud, piercing nicker into the still night. He nickered and waited expectantly with his ears cocked forward, his eyes looking intently out in the shadowy distance. But there was no answer. After a little time Blaze Face sent out another wild nicker and again he waited. He did this the third time, and almost as soon as the echo of this last call died away there came an answering call, a distant nicker from a horse. Blaze Face stood trembling with eagerness when he heard it. And in a few minutes more, although he had made no more calls, he heard again that same nicker. It was coming closer and to Blaze Face it said, "Where are you?" And Blaze Face, understanding perfectly, sent back his shrill call which said, "I am here!"

There was silence for a time. Then some shadows appeared on the skyline to the south and the shadows could be seen moving down on this side of the ridge. Presently they were seen closer still and it wasn't long until the shadows all stood on the plain, only a few rods away from Blaze Face. It was Cinchfoot and the old range horses, and Cinchfoot was leading them. He stood still for a minute and so did all the old horses. Their heads were toward Blaze Face and they were all looking intently at him. Finally Cinchfoot made some low nickering sounds. What he was trying to say was, "Well, well! My old pal, what's wrong that you stay so close there? Come on out here with the rest of us." But Blaze Face only made some more low sounds, sounds that told Cinchfoot how much he wanted to be near him but for some reason could not come away from the place where he stood.

The old horses didn't want to stand still here. They were thirsty. This was the place where they had come for water many times and they didn't see anything suspicious about Blaze Face standing there by the spring. They began to get restless and started to crowd past Cinchfoot. He nipped one or two of them and tried to hold them back until he looked things over a little more, but they crowded right on past him, nipping back at him and squealing a little, too, as if to say to him, "What do you want to stand here for? We're thirsty and we aim to drink!" And presently they stood with heads down, silently drinking the cool water. Cinchfoot stood staring at them. Things looked almost safe here but he was still a little uneasy. He was thirsty. He wanted to drink and also he wanted to go up to Blaze Face. The old horses took plenty of time at the spring. They would drink for a time, then raise their heads, draw a long breath, cock their ears, look up at the hill in front of them and at nothing in particular for a time, then they would put their heads down and drink some more.

Cinchfoot couldn't wait any longer. With his head high, and his eyes trying to see everything, but not able to see much except Blaze Face, he trotted up to his old friend and they talked in their own language for a time. Cinchfoot then drank from the spring and began to look about him. He took a few steps out in the bare place and began to sniff at the ground. He stood there for a second all alone. And in that second some object seemed to jump up at him from the dust like a striking snake. He leaped to get away but at the same time felt something around his feet and before he could realize what had happened he had run hard against a rope; another was around his fore leg now, and he was thrown hard. Before he could get up he saw two men running toward him and then he was up. But in that little time another loop was ready and even as he threw out his front legs to get to his feet the loop settled over his head and Cinchfoot felt it tightening around his neck. He was scared, but like a wise horse of the West, he had learned, like Blaze Face, that there was no use to fight a rope. He leaped to his feet and stood trembling as the two Mexicans came up. They left the one rope tied as it was to the base of a small tree and soon they had Cinchfoot tied to the tree with Blaze Face.

Here these two stood and nosed each other and waited for the next move. And both of them knew they would not get loose when they saw one of the men seat himself on the ground nearby while another hurried toward the pine woods. Presently they saw this man coming back from the woods riding one horse and leading another. Both Blaze Face and Cinchfoot had learned before this that when a rope was fixed around the neck and pulled, they must allow themselves to be led. They both had learned it was best not to fight but they knew also that something might happen to these ropes. And if the ropes once came off, Blaze Face and Cinchfoot didn't need anybody to tell them what to do. The men tied Cinchfoot and Blaze Face together. A long rope was then tied to Blaze Face and Felipe rode forward. Carlos rode behind and so it was that Cinchfoot allowed himself to be led. But he and Blaze Face were glad that, although they were captives, they were still together.

The two riders rode forward steadily. No word was spoken by the men and in the main the only sounds were the steady hoof beats of the four horses on the ground as they moved on in the moonlight. The hills and rough land were avoided and many times it was necessary to go in a wide detour to avoid a ravine or deep coulee. At times, when Cinchfoot lagged a little, he felt the tap of the end of a rope against him and at such times he would jump and trot up very close to Blaze Face. For some time they had passed along on a high plain when all at once they arrived at a steep incline leading to a wooded valley below. A brief halt was made here and the riders talked in low tones. Cinchfoot and Blaze Face stood looking down the incline at the dark pine forest in the valley and neither of them wanted to go down there. When the riders started for-

ward again Blaze Face lunged back and so
did Cinchfoot. But they were securely tied
and after a little they found there was no use
to fight. The rope behind began to tap both
of them again and they lunged forward as far
as they could and so began to descend to the
valley below.

When they were at last down on the level
they found many shadows there. Trees seemed
to be everywhere on both sides of them but an
open space led on and across the valley, which
the riders followed. After a time they moved
out of the wooded valley and in the distance
ahead there suddenly loomed the faint glow of
a small fire. Felipe exclaimed at once, "There!
So our friends come and wait as they say!"
And in due time this proved to be so. The
light in the distance was made by a camp fire,
near which were two riders who were part-
ners in this scheme to capture Cinchfoot and
Blaze Face. After some difficulty Blaze Face
and Cinchfoot were led fairly close to the fire
and the two white men, who had been squat-
ting on their heels near the fire, got up and

walked forward to look at the prizes. One was addressed as Jack, the other as Bob. The one known as Jack said, "Well, so you got both of 'em, and look at this fine black stallion with his silver mane and tail! We know how this Blaze Face horse can buck because we've seen him, and this Cinchfoot will be a wildcat under the saddle. We'll have to take 'em a mighty long way from here but that's easy done because the railroad with its cattle cars goes places a long ways off! You fellers have done a good job of it and now we'll pay you for 'em but our agreement was you'll have to help us to get 'em to the railroad. And you're hungry by now so I reckon you can light and eat."

While this talk was going on Cinchfoot and Blaze Face stood looking at the fire and the men and pulling back now and then as far as they could. They did not like any of the men and they didn't like the strange smells coming from around the camp fire.

The two Mexicans dismounted and sat near the fire and ate in silence. When they had finished they lay down and at once fell asleep.

The other two men waited and at the end of about two hours the sleepers were awakened and all four men mounted and rode forward, Cinchfoot and Blaze Face being led as before. About an hour after sunup the riders halted at some water holes and all the horses were allowed to drink. After this there was no more stopping until mid-afternoon and all the horses were very hungry. But there was only a little time to stop and eat as the riders wanted to make more and more haste to reach some particular point. And as they again all rode along the two white men asked many questions of Carlos and Felipe.

It was after sundown when the riders stopped. They were coming near the small town where they were headed for. The two white men talked for some time with Felipe and Carlos and at last gave them some money. They seemed to be satisfied with the pay and talked on a little longer. As they talked the night fell quickly. The two Mexicans now mounted their horses and rode away.

Cinchfoot was hungry but he was a little

nervous, also, because of the surroundings here. He wondered about the tiny twinkling lights not far away. Blaze Face also saw the lights and he began to stare at them. Cinchfoot moved about restlessly and so did Blaze Face. They were tied to two pine trees some distance apart. Cinchfoot put his nose down to the ground in the hope of finding some grass to eat but his nose found only some cold rocks around him and as he stepped about his hoofs made a clattering sound on the loose rocks. Blaze Face did the same and he got so restless he began to paw the ground with a front hoof.

After more than two hours of waiting Cinchfoot and Blaze Face saw their captors coming up to them and in a short time they were again tied together and led as before, and now they were moving toward the twinkling lights.

In due time they arrived at the edge of a small town which was a shipping point for cattle and horses. Cinchfoot and Blaze Face were first taken through a gate into a corral,

and presently, with Blaze Face first, they were
moved to the cattle chute that led up into a
cattle car. In this stock car were a number of
other horses. Cinchfoot and Blaze Face could
not see them plainly, because of the darkness,
but now and then they could see their forms
as they moved past the open space of the slat-
like stock car.

Cinchfoot and Blaze Face fought against
going up the chute and into the cattle car
with the other horses. They fought so much
that presently two other men came and gave a
hand. Two men stood inside the cattle car and
pulled on the ropes tied to Blaze Face and
Cinchfoot and at the same time a man in the
rear brought a whip down on Cinchfoot. He
leaped against Blaze Face, who in turn leaped
up the chute, and in a minute he and Cinchfoot were both in the stock car. All the other
horses inside were driven to the rear of the car
where they were not tied, but Cinchfoot and
Blaze Face were carefully tied in the front
end of the car and two long poles were fixed
behind them so that even if they broke their

ropes they would still be held in these narrow
quarters. It was known to these men that
Cinchfoot was a strange and devoted friend to
Blaze Face, but what Cinchfoot might do to
strange horses if he was loose with them in a
cattle car was another matter. Therefore he
was tied in the front end of the car, with Blaze
Face tied near him so that each could touch
the nose of the other as they stood in the car.

All this had been done and there was some
brief talk among the men, when they hurriedly began to get out of the car and to fasten
the door behind them. One of them had said,
"There she comes!" He meant the train and
already the whistles of the engine sounded in
the distance.

The freight train thundered in, stopped,
and the engine began to pull away alone to do
the necessary switching here. There wasn't
much to do on this night. Just one car of horses
to get. This car was soon coupled on to the
train and after a little more time for the fire-
man to put water in the boiler of the engine,
there was a loud whistle and a lantern swung

out from the caboose at the rear of the train to tell the engineer to go ahead.

Cinchfoot and Blaze Face found that the queer thing they were tied in was moving steadily, moving forward and at the same time jolting them about as the car lurched sidewise. And added to this was the bother of the loose horses behind that kept coming up, now and then nipping the two that stood tied in the front end. Blaze Face suddenly kicked back and his hoof struck a meddlesome horse. Cinchfoot tried the same and he also kicked a horse that had just bit him, and he kicked the horse so hard on the knee that it limped when it backed away. It was lucky the two poles behind Cinchfoot and Blaze Face were high enough so that they could use their hind legs. Not being able to use their teeth, they could kick the troublemakers. But after a little of this the loose horses got back where they belonged and stayed there. They felt as did Blaze Face and Cinchfoot. They were hungry. But not as hungry as these two because all the other horses had had a good feed of

oats in the afternoon, while Cinchfoot and
Blaze Face had had nothing to eat at all for
many hours.

The train rattled on for a long time. Now
and then it lurched from side to side and there
was a general commotion among all the horses
as they were jostled by the train and thrown
against each other. After a time the train
seemed to strike a level track and the horses
in the rear got quiet. When the train lurched,
Cinchfoot and Blaze Face had to fight to keep
their feet, but they did not try to lunge back
and break the strong ropes that held them.
They were too wise for that. Fortunately they
were tied long enough so that their heads were
free. When the cattle car traveled smoothly
again Blaze Face would put his nose over to
Cinchfoot and these two would exchange
greetings and by this they encouraged each
other.

Sometimes they would try to look out in
the night through the openings between the
slats to see how things looked outside. And,
although they could see through the openings

of the slats of the car, the trees and rocks seemed to be always running past them. After the train had run smoothly for a time the loose horses again began to come up and nip the two tied in front. This brought quick kicks from Cinchfoot and Blaze Face, and after a little of this the loose horses went back in a huddle and pricked up their ears and looked at the two tied in front as if to say, in cowboy language, "Well, ain't they the fightenest horses, them being plumb set on being let alone!"

Finally the dawn began to come and presently it was broad day. Soon the train stopped. In a little while three men walked up to the cattle car where the horses stood. The door of the car was opened and one of the men got in the horse car and brought oats and water to Cinchfoot and Blaze Face. The other horses were also fed and given water. In about an hour the train started on again. And it rattled steadily on hour after hour. Cinchfoot and Blaze Face could see out plainly now and they spent most of their time looking through the openings in the car and wondering when they would get out and so get a chance to run away. They never forgot this part of it. That was the thing that was in their minds constantly.

All that day and all the following night the train moved on, stopping a few times to get water for the engine; then it clattered on and it ran on most of this day also. At last it began to slow down and then it stopped. Cinchfoot and Blaze Face could see many strange sights now. It was still daylight but getting along toward evening. They both looked out on the side where Cinchfoot was tied. Just beyond the train they could see life of many kinds, men and horses and women and children and a vast fenced-in place with small buildings scattered around. The train had backed the car in which the horses were to a cattle chute. This was the end of the railroad journey. Cinchfoot and Blaze Face were to be taken from the cattle car, although they didn't know that as yet. And now many men and boys approached this car and some of the boys began to call to other boys and to talk loudly:

"Hey! Do come and look at this wonderful jet black horse with a white mane and tail! I bet the fellers that tries to ride *him* in the rodeo will get plenty!"

"Yes, and look at this other big black horse with a white face. Ain't he a beauty, too!"

"It's so, and see how they have had to tie these two big ones. Had to *tie* them or maybe they would have busted the car and got out!"

"I sure don't want to miss the show tomorrow. That's when the top riders are going to try to ride these two! Going to let 'em rest up a little, then try to ride 'em. Tomorrow will be a big day here!"

Although neither Cinchfoot nor Blaze Face could understand this talk, it was a fact that they were at last at the end of this strange journey, for they had been bought for this rodeo show and shipped here for the purpose mentioned. Real hard bucking horses were wanted here. It looked as if these two standing in the front end of the car would make excitement enough for the people who bought tickets to see the rodeo.

VIII: *Bucking Horses*

WHILE Cinchfoot and Blaze Face were being taken out of the cattle car many cowboys stood around looking on. One of them said, "Well, the bucking of the horses at this rodeo the last couple of years ain't been any too good but it looks like them two black horses there will buck plenty."

"You bet!" said another. "And especially it looks like that black one with the silver mane and tail would buck more than plenty."

"It's so," another spoke up. "It looks like when a feller gets up in the middle of him that same feller will go so high he'll have trouble finding the ground. But no matter. He'll be tried anyway."

While this talk was going on the new horses were all taken out of the cattle car and in a little time Cinchfoot found himself in a stable beside Blaze Face. The two were in a wide stall together and each was tied with a rope and hackamore, or rope halter. In a short time a good feed of oats was brought in and dumped in the feed boxes. Cinchfoot and Blaze Face were both so hungry it seemed they couldn't eat fast enough. A little later on both were given water and then they were left to themselves for a time. This was pleasing to them. They put their noses together and looked each other over, just saying in their own way that they were glad to be together. And then Blaze Face raised his head and looked about his prison and snorted. It was as if he said, "Well, my good pal, I wonder what they aim to try on us next? Anyway, we're all fixed up for the present!"

Cinchfoot answered by looking about him with wide eyes and giving a loud snort, trying to say, "Yes, they got us for the present but give us a chance and we'll get to new country in a hurry." And so the night passed and morning came.

The rodeo was only a short distance from this stable and pretty soon the crowd began

to gather there for the big show. The rodeo
was the kind that stayed in a town for a week
and the people came from far and near. Already on this day the small town was full to
overflowing with people.

After several hours went by loud yelling
could be heard on the rodeo grounds and now
and then the bawling of a bucking broncho.
The big show was on. The bawling of the
horses out there in the arena made Cinchfoot
and Blaze Face uneasy. They raised their
heads and tried to see out, but not much could
be seen except through the open door behind
them. Occasionally they saw a horse leaping
and bucking with his cowboy rider out on the
level arena. Now and then they saw a cowboy
go up in the air and land on the ground, and
the bucking horse would go right on bucking
as if he hated the saddle so much he wanted to
buck that off too.

But there was good hay in the manger and
Cinchfoot and Blaze Face spent only part of
the time looking out through the opening in
the stable behind them. They would eat a few

mouthfuls of hay and then turn and look back at what was going on out in the arena of the rodeo. The weather was warm and balmy outside, with green trees and green grass everywhere, and a peaceful feeling in the air. And it seemed the people were having a good time out there by the way they shouted and laughed at things generally.

A few times during the day a number of boys came to the door of the alleyway in front of the stall of Cinchfoot and Blaze Face. They went in to look at both of them, but especially they admired Cinchfoot with his jet black coat and silver mane and tail. At such times the boys talked with admiration and awe.

"I bet when a cowboy gets up on one of *these* two he'll know he's been some place!"

"You bet he will, and likely they'll dump every feller that gets on 'em."

"I can hardly wait until tomorrow to see these two come out of the chute!"

"Yes, it's so. When these two come out, we'll see riding that *is* riding."

"Only we'll likely see bucking that *is* bucking!"

But Cinchfoot and Blaze Face didn't pay much attention to the boys. They just looked them over a little, while chewing hay, for they looked small, and people as small as these likely couldn't do much harm. It was the big folks that would have to be watched and bucked off, if they tried anything. Neither of them knew what was going to happen to them here, but they were both suspicious.

The day went by. Cinchfoot and Blaze Face had another good meal of oats at night and the next morning they had still another good portion. They were given plenty of good water, too. About noon Cinchfoot was in such fine spirits he reached over and playfully nipped Blaze Face as if to say, "Well, old pal, how goes it? I feel pretty good! How is it with you?"

Blaze Face replied by nipping Cinchfoot on the neck and saying to him, "I'm feeling plenty good! Mighty good in fact, and if any of that outfit out there tries to get up on me I, personally, aim to go places with that same person!"

Cinchfoot squealed a little and answered, "Yes, and let one of 'em try to set up on *me!* If they do I aim to throw 'em plumb into new country!"

About the middle of the afternoon four cowboys walked into the stable and led Cinchfoot and Blaze Face outside. They did not lead very well. Both of them shied a good deal and it took all four men to get them in the small corral where the rodeo chute was. But presently they got them in. Blaze Face was the first one to be saddled. While this was going on a Westerner in cowboy costume was riding in front of the grandstand and shouting to the big crowd of people that filled all the seats: "Ladeez and Gentlemen! We aim now to bring you a sight you don't see every day. We got two of the wildest bucking horses in captivity! They was as wild as the wildest Indians when the cowboys ketched 'em and we aim to show you some riding that *is* riding! We got with us today two of the greatest riders in the

world which the same is Bill Dirks of Wyo-
ming and Buck Hawks of Montana. The first-
named rider will try to set up in the middle of
the big black gelding horse until the same
quits bucking. No monkey business about this
here riding today! No cowboys will come
along and take either of these great riders off.
They won't need to on account both these
riders have said they will stay on these two
black horses until the cows come home!"

Laughter and good-natured jokes greeted
this from the grandstand. The announcer, riding on a big pinto horse, now turned away
from the people and headed his horse toward
the chute where the "wild ones" were being
made ready. Cinchfoot and Blaze Face had
been taken into the small corral around the
chute, where the buckers had to leap out into
the arena. Blaze Face was put into the chute
first. He fought against this but so many men
were pushing him they had their way. There
he stood for a minute, the saddle on him and a
man sliding down into the saddle from above.
Suddenly the door of the chute was opened

and a wild yell went up from the grandstand. Out popped Blaze Face with the cowboy, Buck Hawks, in the saddle. Blaze Face leaped and whirled and went up and down in a way this cowboy had never seen. Halfway across the arena Blaze Face threw Buck so high there was a lot of space between him and the saddle, and Buck went sailing through the air to strike the ground with a thud.

The yelling from the people on the grandstand was wild and happy. One man yelled, "Now that's bucking that *is* bucking. Let another feller try that horse!" And, although it was unusual, Blaze Face was taken into the chute again and another cowboy slid into the saddle. Out Blaze Face rushed and it was the same thing. Blaze Face threw this rider quickly. Once more he was tried and still again, and before he was done the fifth rider had got on his back. This cowboy managed to stay on but only because Blaze Face was tired out. He was led back to his stall in the stable and tied there alone. At once he let out a loud, shrill nicker for Cinchfoot, and Cinchfoot,

who was now being driven into the chute, let
out a loud answering call to Blaze Face. It
was as if Cinchfoot was yelling, "I hear you,
my friend! They're working with me now but
I aim to show 'em before they're done with
it!" And the men had a lot of trouble getting
Cinchfoot into the chute because Blaze Face
kept nickering wildly to him and Cinchfoot
kept nickering wildly back to his pal. At last
Cinchfoot was in the chute and a cowboy, Bill
Dirks, slid slowly down into the saddle. A gun
was fired for the signal and out he came—a
great jet black horse with a beautiful silver
mane and tail. But there was not much time to
think about how beautiful he was because he
was showing the hardest and swiftest bucking
imaginable. Cinchfoot was somewhat bigger
than Blaze Face. He had longer legs and he
was younger and quicker. As if to give the
crowd "it's money's worth," as one man said,
he leaped and bucked clear across the arena
and close to the low fence in front of the
grandstand before hundreds of people. Clear
down to the small wire enclosure, where the

other bucking horses who had failed to throw their riders were feeding, Cinchfoot took Bill Dirks in the most lively straight bucking Bill had ever known. Near the wire enclosure Cinchfoot stopped and whirled so suddenly that Bill was almost thrown, and when he stayed on the crowd yelled in admiration. But Cinchfoot was only getting limbered up, as the men said. He rushed back along the low fence in front of the grandstand and when he was about in the middle of it he stopped, bucked once high in the air, dropped to his four feet and when he went up again it was with that swift side sweep that no cowboy could withstand. Bill Dirks was thrown clear out in the bare space in front of the people and Cinchfoot looked at him and snorted.

One of the men in the grandstand shouted, "He's saying, 'There he is, folks! Take him if you can use him. *I* sure got no use for him!'" Wild yells of laughter came from the men, and one shouted, "Let some other feller try that horse!"

This was done. Six riders in succession tried

to ride Cinchfoot but he didn't seem to get
tired as Blaze Face had done. He threw all his
men and he threw the last one higher and
harder than the first. This aroused great yelling and cheering in the grandstand and it was
agreed on all hands that both Blaze Face and
Cinchfoot were very valuable rodeo horses
because they would draw a big crowd when
men tried to ride them. And now while other
bucking horses were being saddled and gotten ready for other riders, Cinchfoot was led
out of the arena and toward the stable. And
the crowd turned to look at him as he leaped
and lunged to get away from the men who led
him.

Loud calls from the men in the grandstand
could be heard, such as, "Now *ain't* that a
great horse!"

"You bet he is and such a beauty, too, with
his silver mane and tail. He's the purtiest
horse I ever seen!"

"Yes, and you can see neither him nor his
mate is used to such rough treatment, being
spurred and the like. See how excited he is

now! And his mate was the same. They'll buck worse than ever tomorrow."

What the men said about the effect of rough treatment the riders gave Cinchfoot and Blaze Face was so. The cowboys didn't intend to be especially rough with any horse, but it was the custom when riding a bucking horse to use the spurs on him, as it was believed that this was the way to tame him. But this treatment was new to Cinchfoot and it had been a long time since Blaze Face had known any of it. The reason was that for several summers Clem Brown had been the only rider of Blaze Face, and Clem never spurred him. He learned early that Blaze Face was the kind that went wild if he felt the sharp spurs. He was the kind that could not be tamed that way. More gentle means had to be used with him. And as for Cinchfoot, he had never in his life felt a spur sticking him until this day. Clem Brown even took his spurs off when he mounted Cinchfoot. Clem was a wise horseman. He knew horses better than most men did. And he knew that both Blaze Face and Cinchfoot were the nervous, sensitive kind that could never be tamed by spurs but would be made all the wilder because of such things.

At last Blaze Face and Cinchfoot stood side by side in their big double stall in the stable. Their sides stung and smarted where the spurs had gouged them, and they were both sweating and trembling. But after they had nosed each other and made some low sounds in talking this over, they began to stop trembling and after a little they began to eat a little of the hay that was in the manger in front of them. Often they would jerk their heads up from the manger and look back and out of the open door behind them where there was loud yelling going on. And as often as they did this there was something in the minds of both Cinchfoot and Blaze Face that made them know that if they ever got loose again they would never let any man get his hands on them if they could help it. This was not all thought out as a man would think it out, but it was there just the same, and all that was needed to prove it was a chance to get loose.

Presently several men brought water in buckets and set it down before Cinchfoot and Blaze Face and again that night a good feed of oats was given to each of them. The ropes of their halters were tied long enough so that they could both lie down, and later on when the night was about half over they both did lie down and got a good rest.

Although Cinchfoot and Blaze Face did not know, there were still three more days of the rodeo and a great crowd was expected these last few days because of the two great buckers. And, in particular, everyone would want to see Cinchfoot because it was seen already that he was one horse that no man could ride. At least it was doubtful, and that's what would bring the big crowds.

The next day came and with it a big crowd of men, women and boys. Everybody had heard about the two big black horses that could buck the men off in record time and everyone especially admired the black horse with the silver mane and tail. They said Blaze Face was a beautiful horse, too, but he could not compare with the majestic Cinchfoot. Both the horses had been given new names here. Blaze Face was called the Wasp, and Cinchfoot the Hornet. The rodeo owner did not know their real names.

Along in the afternoon Cinchfoot and Blaze Face were again brought out, led into the pen near the chute, and in due time Blaze Face was announced. He leaped out of the chute bucking with a new determination. This was to throw every rider that got on him, and he did. He tossed off the first man in a few twisting jumps and then he bucked off four others almost as soon as they got on him. Then Cinchfoot was announced. Out he leaped, whirling and bucking, and if Blaze Face got his man off in a dozen jumps, Cinchfoot got his man off in less than half that time.

But at last they were led away and both of them were so worked up and excited this time that it took several men to get them back in their stall in the stable. Then they were tied and left alone for the time. Cinchfoot and Blaze Face had both won a victory, but it had not been easy. In fact it had been pretty "tough," as the western men would say.

Because so many riders with sharp spurs had been on Cinchfoot and Blaze Face, they both felt sharp stings and smarts where the spurs had cut into their flesh, and their sides were cut and bleeding. And what made it worse was that flies were now on their wounds. But being tied by their heads they could do nothing except switch their tails and stamp about in the stall and so relieve themselves as best they could.

IX: *The Hiding Man*

THE next day it was the same. Cinchfoot and Blaze Face were the center of attraction of the whole rodeo, and again Blaze Face threw several riders, and at last got so tired that a rider stayed on him. But not so with Cinchfoot. He again threw every man that got on his back and he leaped so high and bucked so terrifically that he threw all the riders hard. The rodeo owner was delighted. Here was a pair of horses, and one in particular, that would make money for him all over this part of the West, where the rodeo was now showing.

When the rodeo moved away from this town Cinchfoot and Blaze Face were again put in a cattle car with the other rodeo horses, and they were shipped to the next place, and again it was the same. They were both tied by their heads at night in some stable as the owners feared they might break out of a horse corral. And each night both Cinchfoot and Blaze Face felt the smartings and stinging of the wounds the riders had made with their spurs.

As the days went by Cinchfoot and Blaze Face got more and more wild and more determined to get away. Two or three times they did almost get away. But something happened each time and they were still in the clutches of the men. But one thing now was certain. It was that if Cinchfoot and Blaze Face ever *did* get free, they would run wild the rest of their lives if they possibly could. Neither of them would trust a man. Both of them if free would run in terror and, if pushed hard enough, take desperate chances to escape.

However, while Cinchfoot did not realize it, there was nevertheless something away back in his brain that would tell him, if the time ever arrived, that there was one man in the world who was kind and good to him, and that man was Clem Brown. But Cinchfoot had not thought of Clem during all the rough treatment with the traveling rodeo. He had been too much excited and almost constantly he was watching for a chance to escape.

The show traveled on from one town to another, and at each town a great crowd of people came out to see the rodeo, and especially the two "wild horses," as Cinchfoot and Blaze Face were advertised. The treatment they received was almost the same at each show.

So things were until early fall. Then Cinchfoot and Blaze Face found themselves in the southwest country. Here they were kept in a large enclosure all alone. They were given food and water each day, and had the run of a large pen, but they were both restless during these months, and both walked around the fence many times during the day and night hoping they might find a place where they could get out and go free. The country here, even in winter, was not cold and only a long crude shed stood in one corner of the enclosure as a shelter for them.

Sometimes at night, when the lonely sounds of the wind drove through the cracks of the crude shed, Cinchfoot and Blaze Face stood in the shelter together, their heads always close to each other. At such times they would close their eyes and sleep a little as they stood on their feet. And so they would doze and wait for the daylight to come, for it seemed to them that something surely must happen so that they could run away from all this together.

But three years passed and during the three winters they were kept here. The climate here was very good. Sometimes a little snow would fall in the night, but it was not very cold and always it would melt the next day, and almost every day the sun would shine bright and warm. Cinchfoot and Blaze Face had shed their long hair each spring and they were both beautiful with their new, shiny black coats when the show started out. But each spring now, after the long hair was shed, there were some white hairs on the black and shiny sides of both Cinchfoot and Blaze Face where they had been gouged hard in the rodeo with the sharp spurs of the riders.

These three years seemed a long time to

them and, as the time passed, they watched more and more for a chance to get away. At last, during the fourth spring with the show, Cinchfoot and Blaze Face were taken away one morning, and after riding for ten miles or so they were led to a freight train and soon found themselves on the railroad again, traveling.

The train went on for three days, then pulled into a town early one morning, and by noon the usual big crowd was on hand to see the rodeo. And the main thing they all wanted to see was Cinchfoot and Blaze Face in action. The news had come in advance about them and when finally these two leaped out of the chutes with riders on them it was seen that the news hadn't been exaggerated. And again here, as in the other towns, Cinchfoot and Blaze Face were ready to fight the same every day. Each afternoon they bucked the riders off, and now only two days were left of the week for the show here. On the next to the last day Cinchfoot fought as hard as ever and he again tossed his riders high in the air, but by

this time it was seen that Blaze Face was
breaking under the strain. It had been too
much for him, and although he bucked with
the first man and threw him, the next man
stayed on. But Blaze Face had not, by this,
made up his mind to give up and stay with
the men. If he could get a lot of rest he would
fight again. It was simply that he was getting
older and that he would need a longer rest
between his times of bucking if he was to
throw the men as before.

Late that afternoon Cinchfoot and Blaze
Face were tied together in a stable not far
from the rodeo grounds. They rested the best
they could the remainder of the afternoon but,
now and then, they had to switch their tails
and stamp their feet a good deal and make the
usual effort to get the flies away from the
smarting cuts on their sides made by the sharp
spurs of the men. They both wanted water to
drink. They wanted water each day after
these battles with the riders. Their throats at
such times felt hot and dry. But the men who
led them into the stable and tied them on this

day seemed to forget the water, and they hurried back to the rodeo. Two boys, who had secretly admired these two fine black horses, slipped away and presently brought in two full buckets of water and set them in the feed troughs for Blaze Face and Cinchfoot. Then the boys stood back a little. They did this so the two horses would not be afraid to come up and drink. The horses had started back, afraid, when the water was brought in, but when the boys moved well back Cinchfoot and Blaze Face stepped forward and began to drink the water quickly; but while their noses were in the buckets they kept their eyes on the two boys. They would watch everybody because they had reasons, they believed, to be suspicious of everyone around the place. When the buckets were empty the boys took them and went away.

It was dark when a man brought in water and feed. When he had done this he went outside in the night, walked a little distance away and sat down in the dark shadows of some trees and thickets. From where the man sat he could see the rear door of the stable. He had locked the two side doors. He purposely had left the rear door open. It was a warm night and already it was bright starlight. The man had been left here to guard the two horses but he had something else in mind. He had seen Cinchfoot and Blaze Face in action at the rodeo and he was certain he could not ride Cinchfoot. He was too much for any rider but the man believed he could ride Blaze Face, especially after he had had to exert himself so much late this afternoon. So now this guard would be able to accomplish his purpose. He would take Blaze Face and ride into the distant West with him. But he would wait until the whole town nearby had gone to sleep.

Cinchfoot and Blaze Face, of course, did not know of these plans. Through the cracks in the front of the stable they could see some lights gleaming and they could hear now and then a loud shout from some person, but they paid only slight attention to such things. The thing that troubled them was that they were both tied here in the stable and could not get away from this place where they got such rough treatment. But they were together and that helped a great deal. Their sides smarted constantly where the spurs had gouged them, but now that night had come there were no flies around, so Cinchfoot and Blaze Face didn't need to keep switching their long tails.

After a long time had passed the lights began to go out in the small town and soon the only light that could be seen was the one away off in the depot. At this time the wind began to blow against the old barn and it made low, mournful sounds around the corners and through the cracks of the stable. In the darkness, clouds were moving across the sky so that the stars could be seen only part of the time. In the woods nearby a screech owl sent out his lonesome cry. All the houses in the town were dark and silent now and it seemed as if everything was sound asleep except Cinchfoot and Blaze Face.

But someone else was awake. This was the man employed by the rodeo owner, the one who had been hiding there and waiting. All at once he moved out of the shadows back of the stable and approached the place where the two horses were tied in their stall. The man had a long coiled rope on his arm. He opened one of the side doors and walked slowly up to Blaze Face. The man was afraid if he came in behind Blaze Face he might kick. He had noted, during the riding of both Blaze Face and Cinchfoot, that neither of them had tried to kick at a man, but he did not want to take chances. Blaze Face snorted and got back as far as his rope would let him but he could get no farther. The man paid no attention to this and began to work with the end of the long rope. In a very little time the rope on Blaze Face's halter was untied from the manger and fixed to the long rope the man held on his arm. He now tossed the coil of the rope to the rear end of the stable. Blaze Face did not know he was now untied from the manger and he did what any nervous horse might do; he crowded up close against Cinchfoot. This was what the man had thought and what he wanted. He went around to the rear of the stable and with a long stick pulled the loose rope up and got hold of it. Outside he took a half hitch of the long rope on a nearby post and slowly began to pull at the rope on Blaze Face's halter. Blaze Face pulled back but each time the man took up the slack and after a little time Blaze Face found himself outside the stable at the rear door. He leaped back and started to run but he felt that long rope on him and he stopped dead in his tracks. He knew what that rope would do to him if he ran against it. This was what the man expected. He now took his time and after pulling up the slack each time Blaze Face jumped around, he soon had him within a few feet of the post and tied there. After working skillfully the man got a blindfold over Blaze Face's eyes.

It took another fifteen minutes for the man to put a saddle on him and cinch it tight. Then the man took a chance. He slowly untied the rope on the post, slowly gathered it up in one hand and at the same time he got close beside Blaze Face who could see nothing.

Then, quick as a cat, the man was in the saddle and at the same time he jerked off the blindfold. Blaze Face bucked some but not long. He got tired after a little hard exertion because he had bucked hard in the arena of the rodeo that afternoon. This, again, was what the cunning man on his back had planned on. The man turned him about and rode away at a gallop. Blaze Face was now as he used to be, a tamed range horse for the time. But his mind had not changed in the least. He would break away and stay away the minute he was given a chance.

What bothered him now was that he knew he was being taken away from his pal, Cinchfoot. As the man started toward a trail in the creek woods Blaze Face sent out a loud nicker to Cinchfoot and at once Cinchfoot sent out a loud shrill nicker to his friend. And Cinchfoot understood in a vague way that his crony was being taken away in spite of his wish. He lunged back and tried to break his rope, then straightened up, breathed hard, and with his eyes wide, tried to look through the side of the dark stable in the direction where he heard the nicker of Blaze Face. Cinchfoot sent out one wild nicker after another for Blaze Face and he heard an answer again and again until it was fainter and fainter, and he knew it was getting farther away.

Again and again Cinchfoot lunged back and tried to break his rope but it was big and strong, and lunge back as he would, it held. Again and again he let out a wild nicker but only once more did he hear an answering call from Blaze Face and this time it was so faint and far away that Cinchfoot could just hear it and that was all. Cinchfoot didn't know it was called "west." He only knew his friend was going in that direction. It was away off to the west somewhere. Unless Cinchfoot could break away from here he would lose his pal, the one horse he cared for above all others. Cinchfoot was a full-grown stallion, but he was such a friend to Blaze Face that he would tear this stable down to get to him if he could.

All that night he nickered and fretted and

lunged and was almost frantic when he could no longer hear or see Blaze Face.

When morning dawned and the men walked into the stable they found Blaze Face gone and Cinchfoot standing there trembling and covered with sweat due to his struggles. For a minute the men examined him to see if he had been ridden. Then they understood. He was tied just as they had left him. But his mate had been stolen and Cinchfoot had such an affection for his friend that he had fought to the point of exhaustion to get free and go along with him.

The stealing of horses was so common in these days that often it had to be accepted without much protest.

"Well!" said the western man who owned the rodeo. "We've sure lost one of 'em. And looks like this one would be too tired to buck fellers off today. But we'll see, and tonight we certainly got to watch this stallion ourselves. Two of us can take turns and we'll put him in the lot next to the rodeo grounds. We can see everything that goes on there. Too many shadows around here. We can't afford to lose this one."

The men went away and for a time Cinchfoot was left alone. They had given him water to drink and also some oats. He drank the water but he did not eat much of his oats. He had but little appetite now. He kept turning his head and looking out at the rear door. He wanted nothing in the world but Blaze Face.

As the hours went by and Cinchfoot kept turning his head as far as his rope would let him, to look out at the rear door of the stable, he could see that the place out there was filling up with people. He could see some horses a little to one side of the rodeo arena, horses that in a little time would be ready for the cowboys to ride. A short way from where the horses stood Cinchfoot saw some steers. They would be used also to help make the rodeo a big show but Cinchfoot did not know that he, himself, was the big attraction here. All that he knew was that he did not like the place out there where all those humans were, and he knew also that he would fight them as hard as ever if they led him out there and tried to ride him. But he was not much scared of the men. He could take care of himself around those humans. He knew this because he had already proved it. What troubled him was that Blaze Face was gone completely; he could neither see nor hear him. Suddenly Cinchfoot began to send forth such wild, shrill nickers, one right after the other, that at once two of the men from the rodeo walked over to the stable and tried to quiet him. But Cinchfoot snorted loudly at them when they walked in the stable and he kept right on with his piercing nickers for Blaze Face. Then he would stand and with his ears cocked forward, he would look with blazing eyes back toward the rear door and then on each side, but he saw only the silent gloomy stable.

One of the men said to the other, "We'll have to get him out of here or he may get plumb loose."

"Yes," said the other, "we'll put him in a better place, where we can keep our eyes right on him till we're ready for him."

X: *Cinchfoot Is Down*

It was about the middle of the afternoon when Cinchfoot was taken from a small nearby corral in which the two men had put him. As in other towns where the rodeo had stopped, people for miles around had heard about the two big black horses, but especially they had heard about the jet black horse with the beautiful silver mane and tail that stood out in striking contrast to his shining black body. And Cinchfoot was admired because it was known he had been able to throw all the riders that had mounted him.

Finally the gun was fired and again Cinchfoot leaped out of the chute and again he tossed his rider high and far. Time after time other men mounted him. But it was always the same and at last, while the crowd yelled its joy, Cinchfoot leaped and bucked until he had thrown the tenth man. Sweating and quivering and breathing hard, he was led back to his stall in the stable. Cinchfoot heard the wild yells of praise for him in the rear but he did not know what it was all about. It made him only the more nervous and suspicious.

Finally, after he had rested a little, Cinchfoot was taken out of the stable and led past the grandstand. A man walked on each side of him holding a rope tied in his halter. Cinchfoot had been trained to lead so he did not fight this. He walked along with his proud head high, his eyes flashing. The loud words of praise meant nothing to him, although the words were many and enthusiastic:

"Oh, but ain't he a beauty!"

"I'll say he is. Jet black with silver mane and tail!"

"It's so and he's as stout as he's purty, him being that set on throwing all humans."

"Yes, and if they don't watch out somebody will steal him!"

"That's so. They better watch him awful close."

"I hear the thieves already got away with his mate."

"Listen to him, will you! He's nickering for that same mate right now!"

And so he was. Cinchfoot wanted Blaze Face and, thinking he might be somewhere near, he began to nicker wildly and leap about so much that if it had not been for the two men holding tight to the long ropes on his head he would likely have gotten away. As it was some other men ran out and got hold of the ropes and it took several men to hold him and get him back to the stable where they again tied him.

The two men who owned the rodeo planned to leave him here until after he had been given his oats at night; then they would take him out and put him in an enclosure close to the rodeo grounds. There was a small shed there with a bed of hay on the floor. Cinchfoot would be turned into the enclosure and the men would take turns sleeping in the shed and watching him.

They were being particularly careful be·

cause some men who had heard of Cinchfoot were coming to see the show the next day and it was known some riders had bet a large sum of money that they could ride him. But the men who owned Cinchfoot thought all would be well with him if they watched and saw that he was not stolen. They did not think of anything else that might happen to him. That is, not until it was too late. If they had thought they would themselves have fed Cinchfoot his oats that night, but instead they left it to the man who put the oats in the feed box for Cinchfoot right along.

When it was nearly dark two strange men went into the stable without being seen by anyone. In a very short time they came out and disappeared. It was only a little while after this that the man who was to feed Cinchfoot, knowing he was a little late, hurriedly walked inside and up to the oats bin. The man was a little surprised to see the bucket there already filled with oats. "Well," he exclaimed, "I didn't remember it, but I guess I filled the bucket this morning after I fed him. But it's just as well because I'm a little late with his feed tonight." Dumping the bucket of oats in the feed trough for Cinchfoot the man said, "There you are! Eat your oats! You'll need lots of steam tomorrow on account lots of fellers are betting they can set up on top of you!"

This man went away and some time later the men who owned Cinchfoot came in and took him away with them to the vacant horse lot where they themselves planned to watch him for the night. Cinchfoot had finished eating the oats. He had not noticed anything wrong with the taste of the oats. He had been hungry and he had eaten rapidly. As yet he felt no bad effects from his feed, only a slight numbness seemed to be stealing over him.

What had happened was that the two men who had sneaked into the stable had put "dope" in the bucket of oats. They wanted to have Cinchfoot sluggish enough the next day so that some of the riders could stay on him and so win a lot of money. But they guessed wrong in the amount of the stuff they put in the oats. They had put in too much and so it had become a poison.

When Cinchfoot's owner led him out of the stable they thought at the time that he did not try to lunge and get away as he usually did while being led, but they supposed he was tired from his bucking and plunging with the riders on his back during the afternoon.

They took him into the enclosure with the barbed wire fence all around it. This was a good place to keep him safely, they thought. When they had gotten him inside the enclosure they brought in two buckets of water and set them down in the open. They wanted him to have all the water he wanted in case he got thirsty in the night. The two men then went into the small building nearby and made themselves comfortable on the mound of hay there.

They talked for an hour or so and then agreed that one of them might as well go to sleep. In a short time one man was sleeping soundly while the other sat on the hay and looked out at Cinchfoot. He had drunk from a bucket of water and was holding his nose to the ground as if he might be nibbling at the scanty grass and weeds in the place. Some time past midnight the man who had been asleep waked up and the other took his turn at getting some sleep. The moon was up now and Cinchfoot could be seen standing out in the lot in the moonlight, standing very still.

About two hours later, after the second man had awakened and taken up the watch, he saw Cinchfoot standing very still, and presently saw him lie down and lay his head on the ground. The man did not think much about this. Any horse who is tired might lie down and put his head on the ground.

Cinchfoot didn't move after he lay down, and after some time the man watching began to be drowsy. He did not suppose he would go to sleep, but he did. He went to sleep sitting up, and he stayed asleep until daylight. He waked up suddenly and looked around. He saw the other man still sleeping. The first thing he thought about was Cinchfoot. He was afraid someone had stolen him and he was much relieved when he discovered this was not so because he saw Cinchfoot still lying out there on the ground, his head still down also. The man awakened his partner. They went out to Cinchfoot, supposing he would jump up when they got close, but he didn't. He did not even move, not even when they walked up and stood looking down upon him.

One of the men touched Cinchfoot with his foot and said, "Can't you get up?" But Cinchfoot did not move. He lay and looked at the men with eyes that told them something was the matter with him.

One of the men said, "He's sick. Wonder what has happened to him?" After looking at him for a time they did what was frequently done in these days. They began to prod him with sticks to get him on his feet, since it was believed that if a horse had colic, and he could be got on his feet and made to trot, he would get better. The men kept prodding Cinchfoot, and at last he staggered to his feet and started away. One of the men ran, opened the gate, and Cinchfoot went through the opening and started toward the creek woods not far away. He couldn't go fast and the men ran alongside him, urging him to keep moving. They thought it would be good for him if he could get a sweat started. But when Cinchfoot got in the thin woods near the little stream he stumbled to his knees and went down. The men prodded him again with sticks but Cinchfoot paid no attention. He was too sick to care what they did to him.

The men, being experienced horsemen, realized now that he was in a bad way. One of them went over to the town and brought back a veterinarian. By this time others had heard too, and a large number of people came to look at the beautiful black horse with the silver mane and tail. Men, women, young girls and boys—a great many people—came and stood and looked at the sick horse. The doctor took some time to decide, then he said, "I'm sure he's poisoned. I don't know how, but he's got poison in some way. And there's nothing much to do for him. But don't try to make him get up. He's too sick for that. That might take away any chance he's got. The only thing to do is to let him alone. Put a bucket of water near him, then go away and let him alone."

The crowd stood around a long time and looked down on Cinchfoot. The people all admired him and they wanted to do something for him. Several buckets of water were brought and placed near his head. And some thoughtful women brought a lot of small, leafy branches from the trees and covered him so the flies would not annoy him. But Cinchfoot just lay with his eyes closed and did not seem to know what they were doing around him. He had company and lots of it until it got dark. Then most of the people went away and an hour later he was alone, except for the man the owners had left to guard him.

When morning dawned Cinchfoot was still down and again a large crowd of people came. They all stood around and looked down on him, and they said what a pity it was that such a beautiful young horse had to lie here and die. But the veterinarian who looked him over again at this time said, "Well, he's not dead yet. I fully expected to find him dead this morning. I suppose it is possible he may live. There's no way to tell. I see he has drunk some water from one of the buckets here, but he has taken only a little. Well, keep the leafy branches on him to keep the flies away and don't bother him. Just let him be as still as he wants to be."

All that day Cinchfoot lay and he seemed to be in a kind of stupor. Along about the middle of the afternoon the crowd left and he was again alone. It was at this time when the fever was in him that he began to have vague, strange dreams. Cinchfoot was like a dog that dreams and makes little sounds as he dreams, only Cinchfoot, not being a dog, did not make any sounds at all, but in his fevered condition his hot dry mouth moved every now and then and the muscles on his shoulder twitched and quivered. In his dreams Cinchfoot thought he was back again on the ranch and in the big horse corral with Clem Brown. And Clem seemed to be walking up and saying, "Sugar, Blackie! It's good. Come and get it!" And then just as Cinchfoot seemed to be about to go up and eat the sugar from Clem's hand, he seemed to see his old pal Blaze Face, and Blaze Face was snorting loud and he seemed to be saying to Cinchfoot, "Don't do it! I don't trust that person! And don't *you* trust him, and don't trust any human at all!" It was not words that Cinchfoot dreamed at this time, only thoughts and sensations. But these were perfectly clear. And while he dreamed it was as real to him as when a man dreams. Cinchfoot was very troubled in his dreams, for he wanted to go up to Clem and get the sugar and still he wanted to do as Blaze Face wanted him to do, because Blaze Face had been the best friend Cinchfoot had known from the time he was a small colt. So it was an unpleasant dream. Cinchfoot trusted both Blaze Face and Clem. Then all at once Clem seemed to fade away from Cinchfoot's memory and he seemed to be back in the rodeo again fighting and bucking with all his might to get the men off his back, and again he seemed to feel the sharp stings of their spurs as they gouged his sensitive sides. In fact, what made this sensation was that a fly had crawled down among the leafy branches and was biting at one of the wounds in his side made by the spurs of the riders. But unconscious though he was, Cinchfoot made the flesh quiver at the spot and so drove the fly away.

On the second day the doctor said he could not see any change in him. The people of the town came in the morning and fixed the leafy branches on him to keep the flies away and they put a fresh bucket of water close to Cinchfoot's nose so he might drink when he wished. From time to time he roused up and drank a little of the water, but not much.

Slowly the day faded into night and again Cinchfoot was alone in the small creek woods where there was no sound except the gentle murmur of the little stream as it moaned and sighed its way over the pebbles and sands below.

At times sharp pains darted through his head and at times he would start and quiver all over, and once he was half awake and began to realize a little about things around him, but the fever held him in its grasp and he closed his eyes. He dreamed again and this time he seemed to be running with Blaze Face out in the wild places. It was fine to be free and he ran, as it seemed to him, with all his might, and Blaze Face ran hard also. These two were running neck and neck as they used to do and for a little time, in his dreams, Cinchfoot was in the kind of world where he wanted to be. But in his dream his mind moved swiftly from one thing to another. It seemed to him he was again caught by strange men. He seemed to run against a rope and he felt the terrific, cutting shock as he reached the end of the rope and was thrown so hard against the ground that he could hardly get his breath. But always, at last, he seemed to come back to Clem Brown and he could see

Clem walking slowly up to him and saying, "Sugar, Blackie! It's good! Come and get it!" And this was the finest of all with Cinchfoot. Here was a strange and delightful human, one not like any other. When this man rode Cinchfoot he did not have on his boots the things that gouged a horse's side and made him bleed. He just stayed on and did not hurt him. A queer human, Clem Brown, and the finest ever! The material Clem had in his hand when he said, "Sugar, Blackie! Come and get it," was the most delicious food Cinchfoot had ever tasted. And so in his dreams Cinchfoot's mind seemed to wander everywhere, but it always came back to Clem and Blaze Face. Cinchfoot did not know why Blaze Face did not trust Clem and even was afraid of him. But it did not matter. Blaze Face was fine and so was Clem. Even his friend, Blaze Face, could not make Cinchfoot distrust Clem. No one could do that.

All the second night he lay more like a dead horse than a live one. The only life around him now was the wild kind. Once an owl flew silently over him, circled and lighted quietly on a tree above to look down. Presently the owl flew away and a little later a rabbit hopped silently along the ground and stopped to look. But there was no other stir about the woods, not even a breeze stirred in the trees.

It was a little after dark on the third day when Cinchfoot began to feel much better. The people had come and again gone away and this time he was entirely alone when night fell. The man who had been left to guard Cinchfoot was a drunken sot and was spending his time in the saloon instead of out here. As it was, it was fortunate for Cinchfoot that no one stayed to note his improvement, and so on this night he got the chance he had been waiting for.

An hour after dark Cinchfoot raised his head and lay for a time looking toward the creek where he could hear the sounds of running water. The wind had come up and had veered around to the northwest and blew through the woods with a bracing coolness.

Cinchfoot felt a great thirst and the sound of the running water called him. He put his front legs out in front of him and the next minute he was up on all four feet. He drank the water in one of the buckets but it was the sound of the running water below that called him. He started forward. He walked slowly to the edge of the creek and did not stop until he was out in the middle where the water was up to his knees. Here he drank his fill of the cool running water. He raised his head, drew a long breath and all at once he felt starved for food. He made his way to the other side and walked slowly on for some distance to an open space where he found a large area of green grass.

Cinchfoot ate here for two hours. He felt much stronger then and his mind began to be alert. He wanted to get away from this place and he wanted to move as fast as he could. He sensed that those men he had lately been with might come near at any time. He started away, not knowing what direction to take, but moving on. He wanted the wildest places he could find. And his instinct did not fail him. He started traveling straight into the west. He moved on for hours at a walk and now and then he would stop and take time to eat a little grass, for he seemed now to be always hungry.

Cinchfoot did not notice when the clouds began to come, but they became darker and darker and after a time filled the whole sky. Late in the night he noticed that the wind began to rush across the plains around him and then he felt a few drops of rain strike him. The rumble of thunder made him understand a storm was coming but Cinchfoot paid no attention. He did not hunt shelter but traveled on toward the west. It was not long until the rain began to fall. It drove down in great sheets and the water began to pour from Cinchfoot's sides. All at once he found himself near a river flowing between high sandy banks. In a deep cut, or cattle trail, that led down to the water he took shelter. Here he stood in this cut in the bank until the rain was over. The dawn was now at hand and he could see a thin woods across the stream. Again Cinchfoot followed his instinct. It seemed to him that Blaze Face was away off there somewhere in the west. He sent out a loud nicker across the stream for his friend, but there was no answer. Three times Cinchfoot sent out his loud shrill call and each time he stood and looked across the river and waited, hopefully, but there was no answering call, only the sounds of the river, now swollen by the rain, lapping at the sandy shore near the feet of Cinchfoot. Cinchfoot did not know why. It was only that instinct advised him to cross the river. He plunged into the stream and started swimming across to the other side. It seemed to him that was the direction he should go and he must not let the river stop him.

XI: *The Picket Pin*

As Cinchfoot swam he looked intently across the river to the other side. The current carried him down swiftly but he paid no attention to this. He swam at an angle and far down the river he landed on a low sloping bank on the other side. With the water dripping from him he walked up to the green valley above. There he stood for a minute, his great head held high, the wind blowing against his silver mane and tail. Had Blaze Face gone in this direction? Cinchfoot still believed he had, and after looking for a minute, he sent forth a clear bugling neigh toward the west, his call to his pal of the old days. He stood looking, waiting, listening, but he heard no sound. Again and again Cinchfoot sent forth his shrill call, but there was no sign of life around him except a coyote which stood looking curiously at him.

Cinchfoot put his nose down in the green grass here and ate for some time, then started at a rapid walk toward the west. Something seemed to tell him that was the direction for him. After he had traveled about a mile he turned and looked back. He knew that the men who had held him in their power were back there somewhere. And it came to him he had better get a long way from this place as soon as possible. At first he moved at a trot and then, thinking of Blaze Face, he began to nicker and at the same time to gallop. On and on he ran but there was no sign of Blaze Face and not much sign of life except now and then a jack rabbit that jumped up in front of him and raced away. After a while Cinchfoot felt tired. He stopped in a little green valley and drank from a small stream there. He wanted to go on at once but was very hungry again. He began to graze on the green grass but he spent half the time throwing his head up quickly and looking all around him, hoping to see Blaze Face. The wounds in his sides, where the spurs of the riders at the rodeo had cut him, stung and bothered him now and then. The flies began to annoy him by getting on his wounds, but his long silver tail helped him. He had so much to think about he did not pay much attention to his wounds. He was very lonesome and if Clem Brown at this time had come over a ridge and called to him Cinchfoot would likely have gone to him.

But in all this his mind was constantly on Blaze Face. Cinchfoot was not like the average horse: he remembered the friend who had been with him and helped him out of his troubles since he was a three-months'-old colt. He didn't know how other horses thought or felt and he didn't know that this friendship between him and Blaze Face was to be known as one of the great stories of the West. He just knew that right now he was pretty miserable, being out here in these wild places and lost from his old friend. But Cinchfoot had learned to like the company of other horses also and the sight of any horse at this time would have been welcome to him, that is, unless the horse had a man on his back. Cinch-foot had no use for such a combination.

After many days of traveling into the west Cinchfoot realized that he was again in wild places that were like those he had lived in when he was a colt. It seemed to him that Blaze Face should be around here and, time after time, in the daylight hours and some-times in the starlit nights, Cinchfoot would stop his grazing to send out a loud nicker for Blaze Face. But there was no answer. Then late one evening Cinchfoot walked up on a high ridge and saw something that made him stop short. Down on the valley below he saw a log house and a number of horses in a cor-ral near the house. As soon as Cinchfoot ap-peared on the ridge all the horses in the corral raised their heads, looked up and saw him. At once one of them sent out a loud nicker of welcome. Cinchfoot was about to nicker in return but he saw two men come out of the house and start walking toward the horses. Then the two men saw the great black horse with the silver mane and tail standing proudly up on the ridge. They stopped in their tracks. Certainly, they thought, there was a horse worth getting if they could manage to do the job. While the men stood looking at him some of the horses in the corral kept nickering in a friendly way to Cinchfoot.

It was getting late. The sun was down and already the shadows of evening were coming over the place. In a few minutes it would be dark; in the West the dark comes quickly a little after sundown. These men knew this. They were horse rustlers and it was necessary for them to know the time of daylight and dark. But Cinchfoot did not know what kind of men were here. He did not know that this was an old abandoned log house and that the old corral where the horses were was in pretty bad shape, that it would not have held the horses if they had run against it. But all the horses in there had been thrown with ropes and they were afraid to run against anything near them that even resembled a rope. Cinchfoot didn't know about all this. All he knew was that horses down there in the corral were his kind of company and he wanted very much to go to them. But at the same time he didn't want the men to get hold of him. He was free. He expected to remain so.

The two men looked up at him for a minute, then turned and walked back to the log cabin and went inside. They had gone to the house to get their ropes so they could be ready when Cinchfoot should come up in the darkness to the other horses. They were certain he would do this because the horses kept nickering to him and presently they heard Cinchfoot nicker to the horses. It was already getting dark and presently it was, as the cowboys would say, "plumb" dark. The two men picked up their lariat ropes. As they did this one of them noticed a picket pin on the end of his rope. This picket pin was made of a sharpened stake of wood, such as was used in the West at the time, to drive into the ground and tie a horse to when he was grazing. He had left the picket pin there for two reasons. It was a good picket pin and the rope was on very tight. It had got wet dragging in a river

they had crossed that morning. So, being in a
hurry, the man left the picket pin as it was.
The two men wanted to get the ropes and so
find a good hiding place out near the old
horse corral and the picket pin on the end of
the rope was hardly thought of. Both men
went out in the dark with their coiled ropes
on their arms. In quick time they got under
the deep shadows of some trees near the corral where they waited.

In the meantime Cinchfoot had worked his
way along the ridge to a point north of the
log house and he began to move watchfully
toward the horses that kept nickering to him.
Now and then he walked under a tree which
cast its dark shadows over the ground and
each time he stopped in the shadows and
looked forward. He was looking for some
sign of the men, but none was to be seen.

Cinchfoot spent some time in coming up to
the corral, and when he got close he waited
again. But the two men watching him had the
patience of wild animals, watching and waiting for their game. The men thought Cinch-

foot was a beauty worth waiting for. At last Cinchfoot stood only a few yards from the horses. The old corral that held them was not high. The horses inside could put their noses over the top poles and they did this while talking in their own language in low tones to Cinchfoot. It was horse language telling him he might as well come on up and get acquainted, that he could see that *they* couldn't go to him. Not that they didn't *want* to go to him. They did, but they couldn't just at this time, and so why wouldn't he come on up and be friendly? That was what all the low sounds of the horses meant to Cinchfoot. There were a dozen of them in the corral and after they all began to make these friendly sounds, Cinchfoot forgot about the man and walked up to the corral and began to put his nose up to the horses to say "howdy."

Things were going very well with the introductions here and Cinchfoot had wholly forgotten the men. He was talking to the horses now and he was telling them they might as well come and go along with him, it being unnatural for them to be penned up here. "Come along and let's go!" Cinchfoot was urging them. But it was no use. The horses did not know any way to do this. It took an accident to show them how.

Suddenly both Cinchfoot and the horses in the corral were startled to see two human forms dart out from the shadows and on either side of them. At the same instant two ropes hissed through the air toward the head of Cinchfoot. One of the ropes missed; the other loop fell over his head. But Cinchfoot leaped and rushed so hard he jerked the rope out of the man's hands before the man could get set for the shock. At the same instant the horses in the corral, scared frantic, rushed in a mass against the opposite side of the old corral, crashed into it and before they knew it they were all out and running free.

Cinchfoot ran with them, the long rope on his neck trailing behind him and now and then causing him to stumble a little as his front foot stepped on it. But even so he was able to keep up with the running horses and

the horse rustlers were left to make the best of
their loss, not only of their stolen horses, but
their saddle horses which had also been in the
corral. But neither Cinchfoot nor the other
horses knew that the men could not pursue
them. They supposed they could and they ran
on for many miles. It was fine, they all felt, to
be free again.

At times the other horses ran ahead of
Cinchfoot because the long rope, dragging
from his neck, hindered him. Now and then
he stepped on it with his front hoofs and was
stopped for a second by the pull of the rope,
and once he got a scare when the picket pin
caught in some brush while he was running
hard. The picket pin was jerked loose but the
taut rope, suddenly released, caused the picket
pin to fly forward and strike Cinchfoot. He
leaped forward and ran the harder. In this
way he kept up with the other horses until all
of them were tired and ready to stop for rest.
They had galloped down a low hill to some
level ground where, by common consent, they
halted and began to drink at some water holes

in one of the low places. Here and there near these water holes grew small brushy thickets and the ground was somewhat stony, so that the grass was not as good here as it was a little farther away. The horses, after drinking, scattered out over the green places and began to graze. Cinchfoot was so hungry he began to bite off the meager grass close to the water holes and as he moved slowly from place to place now and then he stepped on the rope and it bothered him. But he got his foot off it each time and paid no more attention. This rope around Cinchfoot's neck held danger for him because it was a slip noose. If it was pulled hard and *continued* to pull, it would choke him. Cinchfoot did not know this. He knew only that the rope was on him and he did not know how to get it off.

All seemed to go well enough for a time. Cinchfoot had not gone far from the water holes while grazing and he, like the other horses, walked up to the water every now and then to drink. It was nearly dark the next day when Cinchfoot walked to one of the drinking places and drank longer than usual. He then started grazing nearby and after stepping on his rope a few times he raised his head and started off toward the bluff where he had found better grass. But something stopped him. And it wasn't his foot on the rope. The pull of the rope this time was on his neck. He pulled a little once, but only a little, for he felt the rope tighten on his neck. While Cinchfoot had been slowly moving forward, grazing as he moved, the picket pin had dragged along and by accident it had caught firmly in the base of a thicket in such a way that it would not pull loose. If he had not been trained to ropes he might have choked himself by running against the rope, but he did not do this. He pulled a little, then quit and backed up a few steps. The loop slackened and he was satisfied to stay where the rope would not tighten on his neck. But he didn't start to graze right away. He knew something had happened here and, being a smart horse, he was bothered. He knew that in some way he was caught. The rope was fast.

Cinchfoot being a horse could not figure out *how* the rope had got fast. He knew only that it had. And he tried to do his best by not pulling against it.

Cinchfoot tried to go on grazing for a time but each time the rope pulled on his neck he stopped quickly, backed cautiously a few steps, then stood still and looked troubled. Two things had happened that made him very uneasy. One was that the rope had caught on something and the other thing was that he did not dare to pull on the rope, at least not much, for the minute he did, he felt the rope tighten around his neck.

But Cinchfoot was too hungry to stop eating. As long as he kept the rope slack he could graze as well as ever. He watched this part of it and went on eating, but he didn't have much territory to graze in and, after biting off the grass in this small place for some time, he began to wish he could move farther away. The one lucky thing for him here was that he could still reach the water. He walked back there and drank twice on this night. Then he went on nibbling the very short grass that he had already picked over and tried to satisfy his hunger.

The other horses had gone farther away. All of them were getting their fill of grass. Now and then one of them would come up to the water for a drink but this was as close as they got to Cinchfoot. On one occasion a horse walked up to the water for a drink while Cinchfoot was there. Cinchfoot and the horse both had their heads down drinking at the same time. The other horse raised his head first and it happened that his head was under the rope on Cinchfoot's neck. The free horse got scared and leaped backward and, fortunately, he got loose. This was another danger for Cinchfoot that he did not know. If one or more of the other horses should come up to the water to drink at the same time he did, they might possibly get tangled up in the rope. The night wore on and all went well except that Cinchfoot was still held captive by the rope that was fast at both ends, one end on Cinchfoot's neck, the other on the picket pin that was jammed tight at the base of the thicket. When the morning came he began to be hungry. There was no more grass in the small area within the limits of the rope. And even though he walked about here and there, he had been lucky in that he had not got the rope wound around the thicket.

As the time passed he became more and more hungry and he tried to walk very slowly toward the green grass that lay a little beyond. He seemed to think that if he walked very slowly perhaps the terrible rope would no longer stop him, but the thing still held and always it seemed like a thing alive, ready to tighten and bite around his neck. Each time that happened he would stop and look long-ingly at the grass, just look and long for re-lease. That was all he could do. The picket pin was wedged under the thicket as tight as ever.

XII: *The Nicker of a Horse*

WHEN evening of the next day had come Cinchfoot had eaten every blade of grass there was in the small circle around him. In the evening of this day the other horses crowded around the water holes and exchanged the customary squeals, bites and kicks to show they had had plenty to eat and were feeling well and natural. When they had all the water they wanted they stood near the water holes and looked some time at Cinchfoot. It was a puzzle to them why he stayed in one place. But they couldn't figure it out and as the grass was good a little distance away they all went back to their grazing. They would have left him and traveled on but there was no natural leader among them. They stayed close to him because they had a feeling that Cinchfoot was a leader, and if he should go away they might follow him.

During the early part of this night Cinchfoot lay down and rested for some time. But he didn't stay down long. He was too hungry. He spent most of the night trying to find a little more grass and when he got tired of this he rested standing up. When morning dawned the circle where Cinchfoot had grazed looked as bare as the ground around the water holes. Still Cinchfoot kept trying for something to eat. He got his nose close to the roots of the bushes where the picket pin was caught. He nibbled here for a while and bit off some of the ends of the bushes and so the time went on. Three nights and days passed. He was beginning to feel starved and began to eat all the twigs of the brush, even the larger ones with no leaves at all. The twigs were bitter to his taste but he was starving. He was growing weak, too. The other horses kept grazing farther and farther away. They would come up to drink two or three times each day. Sometimes, when they had gone too far away, Cinchfoot would nicker to them. He was trying to tell them he was in bad shape, but they couldn't understand when he nickered; they would only raise their heads from the grass and look at him, but that was all.

During all this time Cinchfoot did not once try to fight the rope. He did pull a little now and then, just a little, when the rope caught on the outer part of the bush but he was careful not to pull on the·loop around his neck. It had made him know what would happen if he did.

At last Cinchfoot got so hungry he seemed about to eat all that bush he could chew on. After he had bitten off some of the larger twigs he pushed his nose down close to the roots to get every last blade of grass growing there. And while he was pushing his nose under the bush a queer thing happened. The loop, which had at the time become quite loose, fell from his head, and lay upon the ground. Cinchfoot, a little startled, jerked his head up—and he was free! He blinked his eyes, looked at the rope for a second, then shook himself, shook himself all over and

ended by tossing his head. He knew the thing
had gone and that he was free!

The first thing he did was to walk to the
water hole and drink a little. He was too hungry to take much time here. He started off, a
little wobbly, toward the grass. The other
horses were grazing quite a distance off but
Cinchfoot did not wait to reach them. As soon
as he got a foot beyond that bare circle, where
he had been held so long, he began to eat for
all he was worth. It didn't matter to him that
the other horses had picked this grass over
and left it. He ate so fast he got some dirt and
sand with the grass but he hardly noticed this.
All the rest of that day and that night he
gorged himself with grass. Along toward
morning some of the other horses walked up
to him and began to nose him but he laid his
ears back and said in his own way, "Don't
bother me! I'm way behind time on all this.
Keep away. All I want is room on green grass
and plenty of it."

Three days and three nights Cinchfoot
grazed in the valley here with the other

horses. It was toward evening of the following day that he raised his head and nickered long and loud, nickered for his lost friend, Blaze Face. He hadn't forgotten him. Cinchfoot was just starting to graze again when he heard faint and far off the answering nicker of a horse. Up went Cinchfoot's head. He listened and waited. Again he heard that faraway nicker. His eyes blazed with hope. Cinchfoot bugled again and his nicker was louder and deeper than that of the horses around him. It was the wild, shrill neigh of a powerful stallion. Once more he held his head up, listening intently. Again he heard the distant nicker and this time it sounded a little nearer. All the horses had their heads up now, listening. Cinchfoot started toward a low ridge of hills in the west. The other horses followed. Again the nicker of the strange horse sounded and again Cinchfoot answered. The horse was coming nearer. There was no doubt about it. Cinchfoot started at a gallop, nickering as he ran, for he had recognized that nicker in the distance.

It sounded again while Cinchfoot ran, and then there was no sound except that of Cinchfoot's pounding hoofs. Suddenly in the distance on the ridge a big black horse appeared. He stopped for a second. So did Cinchfoot, and then with a shrill, glad sound the horse on the ridge thundered down the slope toward Cinchfoot and Cinchfoot couldn't wait. He rushed toward the horse, for he recognized his friend of other days, Blaze Face! These two came together and they made as many sounds as two humans might who had been eager to find each other. Their talk was all in the horse language, low whinnying sounds, and at the same time they put their noses together and looked each other over. Blaze Face seemed to be saying, "Well, so here you are at last! I've been hunting for you ever since that human snared me and rode me away. But here I am and here you are! No matter now. We've got each other again!" And Blaze Face nipped Cinchfoot a little to show he was very much alive, and Cinchfoot, by way of answer, playfully nipped Blaze Face.

When the greetings were over Cinchfoot turned and looked back at the dozen horses who had come up pretty close. They stood with their heads up, looking wonderingly at the two big black horses and especially at the new one with the blaze face.

Blaze Face stood looking at the strange horses for a second, then he walked up to them, looked back at Cinchfoot, and looked at the horses again as if to say, "Well! Who's this you got here? New company it seems. They don't seem very social. I'll get acquainted with them!" Blaze Face walked up to one of the horses and put his nose up to get acquainted. The horse suddenly kicked Blaze Face in the ribs. Old Blaze Face's ears went back and he whirled and slammed his hoofs against the horse. These two kicked a few more times, then the horse snorted and ran off, showing he was well enough acquainted with Blaze Face. Blaze Face then began to nose the others as if to say, "I'm a little surprised at such a reception from one of your number; still, I aim to oblige when necessary. But I want to get on with you, seeing the finest horse in the world, which is my friend, has brought you along with him." Blaze Face all at once seemed happy. He rushed in a big circle around the small herd of horses while Cinchfoot stood off and looked on. After Blaze Face had stopped and snorted Cinchfoot got so happy he raced around the horses, also. He dashed around in a big circle and came to a halt beside Blaze Face. When these two snorted together the other horses seemed to understand everything. They were all free together. There was an instinctive feeling in each of them that at last neither ropes nor hands nor the gouging spurs of men could touch them. All the horses began to run in a circle, shaking their heads and some of them squealing in their new found freedom. After this Cinchfoot started off at a gallop toward the west, Blaze Face right behind him, and the other horses running close in the rear.

When two days had passed and Cinchfoot and Blaze Face had traveled farther and farther into the wild places, the other horses began to drop behind, and after a time they could not be seen. They were range horses and and did not want to get too far away from the places where they would now and then see other range horses. That was natural for them. But Cinchfoot and Blaze Face were different. They hated so much to have men get hold of them that they wanted to go in the wild and stay there. Because of this they wandered on until they reached some of the wildest places in the West. At last, one morning about sunup they saw some other horses, a herd of a hundred or more with a big stallion guarding them.

Cinchfoot and Blaze Face did not know that these were wild horses but it made no difference to them. They decided they would get acquainted and they walked out of some timber and scrub and on across the valley toward the horses who stood with heads up, looking sharp.

Suddenly the wild stallion, a big bay, leaped out and rushed toward the newcomers. He reached Blaze Face first and set his long, dangerous teeth in that horse's neck before he could get away. But all of a sudden the wild stallion found he had bitten off more than he could chew, as the cowboys used to say. Blaze Face wrenched loose and charged in with his long, gleaming teeth. He got a good hold, too, one that cut into the hide of the wild one at the shoulder. Cinchfoot decided now that it would be well for him to get in on this. He got a hold on the wild stallion's neck, close to his ears, and at that instant Blaze Face whirled and sent both his hind hoofs against the stallion's ribs so hard that he almost lifted him from the ground. As Cinchfoot and the wild one reared up and with ears laid back dived for each other again, Blaze Face rushed against the wild stallion and knocked him to his knees. The wild one might have been done for here, but he leaped up and rushed off with Cinchfoot and Blaze Face racing along on each side of him with their ears back and biting his neck like hounds running a wolf and chewing at his neck to bring him down. But the wild one was swift and, as one of the cowboys would have said, "he uncorked some new speed he didn't know he had" and he got away. He stopped fully two miles off, turned, looked back and snorted in wonder as if to say, "Well! I've had tilts before with such as disagreed with me but I never met two such hornets before. They're plumb disgusting! Well, I'll just edge up as close as it seems safe to do and sort of hang around the edges, so to speak; it's lucky I got four good legs!" After this the stallion kept his distance.

This was the beginning of the days with the wild horses. Cinchfoot and Blaze Face roamed with them, and Cinchfoot led them. And it wasn't long until the ranchmen in this region began to complain that a big black wild stallion with silver mane and tail was running off all their range horses. And there was some truth in this. Cinchfoot not only wanted to be free but he believed all other horses should be free, also. Blaze Face agreed heartily. Cinchfoot remembered how the men at the rodeo had hurt him with their spurs and how a rope had held him near that water hole, a rope a man had thrown over him.

But this only brought more trouble for Cinchfoot. Angry ranchmen began to try to run him down. At first it was supposed this could be done if enough riders and horses were in the hunt. But after a month had gone by and three of the ranch outfits had tried this and failed, it began to look as if more trouble was coming for Cinchfoot. One angry ranchman suggested bringing long range guns into play, but after a council this was given up. He was too beautiful, the others said, to be killed like a wolf. Maybe some way could be found to get him alive.

It was early one spring when this conversation took place. The ranchmen supposed that Cinchfoot was a wild horse, since no one had ever been close enough to see the brand on him. They knew Blaze Face had been a saddle horse, for some of them had seen saddle marks on his back. But nothing was thought of that because it was known Cinchfoot had driven away many of all kinds of range horses and it was supposed he had also taken the big black gelding, Blaze Face.

Then as the spring passed the cowboys made a discovery. It was that the great black stallion with the silver mane and tail seemed to be mighty good friends with the big black gelding with the blaze face. No matter what time of day a distant rider saw the herd of wild horses, these two were always close together.

Three times during this summer the range men got near enough to the wild horses to see how the black stallion with the silver mane and tail took care of the other horses. On the instant an alarm was sounded by him, or by Blaze Face, the herd started running. Blaze Face, it was noted, took the lead, while Cinchfoot ran behind to see that no horse stopped by the way or rushed off in another direction.

During this summer various tricks were tried in an effort to catch Cinchfoot. Wire fences were built out from a pocket canyon and, when all was ready, twenty riders tried to run Cinchfoot and his herd into the trap.

But he was too smart to be caught in this way. He rushed to the head of the running horses himself, and led them in a new direction off to the south where the riders could see Cinch-foot and Blaze Face, in the far distance, moving up a steep hill to the timber-covered highlands above.

A number of times the range men tried to run Cinchfoot down by using many horses and changing to fresh mounts. But it was no use. When, after hours of running, he saw that the men would surely come close to the other horses, he would rush away at astonishing speed and vanish into the rough country to the north. The wise old Blaze Face, at such times, left the herd much sooner than Cinchfoot and ran away like a lone wolf to hide until the hunt was over. But later they both would return to the herd.

The summer passed and when late fall came Cinchfoot led his herd farther to the south. But when the winter was over he again longed for the country to the north that was like the country in which he was born. So, when the leaves began to get green on the willows and cottonwoods along the streams, he and Blaze Face led the horses back to the green valleys and clear running streams in the north.

This time Cinchfoot was in for more trouble than he had ever known. He reached this country just in time to drive off a small herd of range horses on the ranch of a big cattle-man who had heard stories about Cinchfoot. It had been told that he had driven off hundreds of range horses over a wide territory and that a certain big black gelding with a blaze face was always with him.

But Cinchfoot had now learned what it was to be hunted. He knew he did not dare to remain long on one range. He knew that after he had had his herd for a time in some fine green valley, he would sooner or later have to leave suddenly because riders would start trying to run him down. And after he had lived a long time in the wild, leading wild horses and range horses he had taken with him, he found that a rider now and then shot something from a distance that caused the dirt to fly up very

close to him. And always there was a loud
crack just before the thing kicked up the sod
close by. Cinchfoot did not know how this
was done. He did not know that the riders
were not shooting directly at him, but only
close so as to make him turn and run where
they wanted him to run, toward some trap
they had laid. But he was always too cunning
to be caught by this.

For three years he led his band toward the
south when the winters came but with the
coming of spring again he drifted north.
Many riders tried various schemes to capture
him during this time but all efforts failed. At
last so many riders began the dangerous prac-
tice of trying to "crease" Cinchfoot that a
wealthy cattleman in the region where Cinchfoot came this spring offered $2,000 for him
if he was caught with a rope or driven into a
trap corral and delivered in good shape except
maybe with a few rope burns on him. And the
cattleman gave orders that none of his riders
should again try to crease Cinchfoot. "Creasing" meant trying to shoot only the top of the

neck of a horse and so stun him until he could be caught.

This stopped the attempts at creasing, but those attempts had already caused Cinchfoot to leave this part of the country. It was terrible to him to hear those rifle bullets whining so close to his ears and once a bullet cut the skin from the top of his withers. This was, as the cowboys would say, "a mighty close call." And Cinchfoot felt that it was terribly close, too. He at once left this region and led his band, Blaze Face with him, to a place known at the Twin Mound country.

Strangely enough, this was the first time in all his three years in the wild that Cinchfoot had traveled far enough to the north to come near the range he had known as a little colt. But on this occasion when he finally stopped in a place that seemed safe enough he knew he was in a region that at least *looked* like the one he had known as a little colt. And Cinchfoot was like a man seeing familiar scenes that looked like those he had known long ago. For to a horse, six years is a long

time in his life. A horse is old when he is fifteen. A boy is just beginning then, but the
horse at that age is old and looking toward
the "West." And so Cinchfoot had already
spent a long time, six years all told, away from
his old home.

Blaze Face had been a mature horse when
he left the old home ranch and now he was
pretty old for a horse and he was at last beginning to feel his age, although he still had
lots of the old fire when necessary.

On this afternoon, when Cinchfoot and the
horses stopped to graze, he didn't think about
going back to Clem. It would take something
unusual to make him want Clem again. Maybe
something pretty bad would have to happen
to bring those two together again. But Cinchfoot didn't think of this. And the truth was
that while the place he was now grazing in
did look like the old home range where he was
born and raised, it was still a long way off to
that range. All unconsciously he was heading
in that direction but, as yet, he was in a strange

country and in territory unknown to Clem Brown.

So, all that Cinchfoot knew was that he wanted lots of good green grass to eat and plenty of water to drink, and he wanted to be free. In the same way he wanted every other horse he saw to be free. He was far from being like the common run of horses. He was like a man in a thousand, who isn't satisfied and happy until everyone else is satisfied and happy. That's why he kept taking the captive range horses away with him. Some of them would stay and others would drift away but Cinchfoot had about a hundred or more horses with him most of the time. And Blaze Face was close to him night and day. That old gelding had things as he believed they should be. There was no man in the world that could ever make him want to be tame again! But Cinchfoot was different. He was different from Blaze Face because there was one man Cinchfoot liked and trusted, and only one.

It was one evening near sundown that Cinchfoot was sighted by a cowboy. And that night this cowboy rode in to a ranch and said, "I expect you fellers have heard of that big black stallion with the silver mane and tail that runs wild with other wild ones. Well, I saw him today with his herd down in a little valley not far from the canyon west of here. I saw him but I'm sure he didn't see me and as I was coming this way I concluded I'd tell you fellers so you can try your luck at getting him. There's a nice natural trap there by the canyon. He and the other horses were grazing in that trap when I saw them. Two high hills are on each side of the place, and if you fellers work it right, you *might* rope him."

XIII: *In the Canyon*

CINCHFOOT had not the slightest hint that night, as he grazed in a narrow valley, that he had let himself into a trap. A natural one it was, not made by men, but one nevertheless that was even better suited for their purpose.

This narrow valley lay between two very steep hills, so steep that a horse must go very slow if he were to get up at all. Both these hills ended at the edge of a deep canyon on the west with a narrow but deep stream flowing at the bottom. About a mile toward the east, the hills fell away into some burned timber land that was a maze of fallen, dead trees. Cinchfoot, Blaze Face and the other horses had come into this valley by moving slowly down the steep hills on either side. At the west end of this valley, where the canyon was, a slope extended clear down to the floor of the canyon where the stream was flowing.

This place was so steep that a nimble and sure-footed horse might get down but he certainly never could climb up. And no horse, unless he was wild with fear, would even attempt to descend into the canyon.

All seemed well in this green valley to Cinchfoot and the other horses. They had no warning of danger until about the middle of the afternoon on the second day of their coming here. And when it appeared it was so bad there was no chance for Cinchfoot to escape except by a hazardous undertaking. The first thing he and the other horses knew was that the valley to the east seemed alive with mounted men. At the same time half a dozen riders appeared on top of the hills on either side to prevent Cinchfoot from trying to climb up the steeps in that direction. And to his consternation, and that also of Blaze Face, a man on foot now suddenly walked out in the open at the west end of the valley, at the edge of the canyon. This rider had, at great pains, left his horse and made his way on foot along the canyon's edge. The man held a rifle in his hand. This was to try to frighten Cinchfoot if he should try the desperate plan of going down into the canyon here. It was not thought that he would try it, but in case he did, the men had agreed that he could be turned back by firing the gun from this point.

When the mounted men suddenly appeared, Cinchfoot and all the other horses stood for a second as if frozen in their tracks. Then Cinchfoot and Blaze Face leaped forward together as if to try to rush by the many riders now coming toward them with loops ready for the cast. Both Cinchfoot and Blaze Face were running hard and all the wild ones were rushing behind. Suddenly Cinchfoot stopped. He stopped so violently he went back on his haunches. The men were almost upon him and in the excitement they actually let Blaze Face rush past them. Every eye was on Cinchfoot. He whirled, looked once hopelessly up at the men on top of the bluffs, then ran with all his power toward the west end of the valley where the lone man stood with the rifle. Crack! crack! crack! the rifle popped, but Cinchfoot was terrified by the riders coming behind him. At last the man with the gun tried a desperate thing: when Cinchfoot was almost upon him he leaped aside so as not to endanger the on-coming horsemen and fired, giving Cinchfoot a flesh wound in the hip, hoping to turn him back. It was not a bad wound, only a slight scratch, but Cinchfoot, terror-stricken, shot past the man holding the rifle, and the next minute the men were all at the rim of the canyon looking down at the great black stallion with the silver mane and tail as he took the dangerous steep. He was sliding on his rump more than half the time but he kept his balance and they saw him at last far, far down on the canyon floor by the water's edge. While they looked they saw him turn his head and look upward at them, then they saw him move along the edge of the water and pass from sight beneath a jutting cliff far down near the water's edge.

The men stood looking for a time but saw no more sign of Cinchfoot. Presently they mounted their horses and rode back to the

east end of the bluffs and at the end of an hour
they were riding in a long line near the canyon toward the south. At times some of them
got off their horses and walked close to try
to get a glimpse of the canyon but it was so
irregular they could see only a little of the
floor of the canyon here and there. They saw
no sign of Cinchfoot. At last, wondering how
he could possibly live down there, they
mounted their horses and rode away.

In the meantime, Cinchfoot had found a
good resting place under the jutting cliff down
in the canyon. He stood on some dry ground
several feet above the river and all was quiet
here except the lapping of the stream against
the edges of the rocks below him. Although
the sun was still shining above, it was well
down in the west and already it was beginning
to grow dark in the canyon. Cinchfoot was
breathing easier now but he wanted to rest,
and he lay down on the dry ground under the
shelf of rock. He was afraid to be down here.
He did not as yet know how he would get out
but he was wise and something told him not to

try going down the river in the dark. Daylight would be the time for that. So he did not move from under the rock. He stayed there hour after hour and waited. Sometimes he closed his eyes and went to sleep for a few minutes, but he was in such a bad place he couldn't sleep long. He was troubled about how he was going to get out. It seemed there wasn't much in being free if you had to be scared stiff most of the time and if you had to be in such a place as this, far down this deep, dark canyon where you didn't know when or how you would get out—if ever. As Cinchfoot dozed his head sometimes dropped lower and lower until his nose almost touched the ground, when he would wake and jerk his head up, scared but not knowing what scared him.

When he woke up like this he would lie still and just look out on the surface of the dark river, but he could see nothing much but the dark. He could hear the water lapping and complaining against the rocks nearby as if the river wanted to take the rocks and everything else clear away from this place. And these sounds went on all through the long night.

When it was morning Cinchfoot got up. He took one look up the steep place he had come down. No use to try to go up there. At once he started down along the edge of the river. Farther along the stream covered all the floor of the canyon and he had to swim. It was a long distance to the next point where he found a narrow margin by the river on which he could rest and then walk a little along the edge of the stream. Again he plunged in the water and again he swam a long distance. He kept this up until late in the afternoon. He would swim along for a time, then he would look for a place along the edge of the stream where he could stop and rest. After resting a while he would plunge in the water again and swim on.

It was nearly sundown when at last he emerged from the canyon that ended in a level valley, and he splashed out to the welcome grassland. After he had grazed here for a while he began to feel very lonely. The way toward the north seemed to invite him. Cinchfoot did not know why. Maybe it was because the land was more open in that direction and grass seemed to be plentiful. Or perhaps in some way he had an instinctive feeling that in *that* direction lay the old home range where as a little colt he had played with Blaze Face. In any event that is the direction he traveled and he traveled steadily except at such times when he stopped to graze on the satisfying green grass.

All that night he moved on and all the next day until it was past noon. He began to be so lonely now that he sent forth his shrill bugle call for his horse companion, the horse above all others for him, old Blaze Face. But Cinchfoot did not see any horses at this time nor until several days had passed. All this time he had been traveling, sometimes toward the northwest, but mainly, straight into the north.

Early one morning when the sun was creeping up over the eastern ridges Cinchfoot saw a number of cattle. This was pleasing to him. He had grown up around such creatures. It was at the foot of a high hill where he first saw the cattle. He stood and looked at them for a time, then, because they were some kind of company at least, he began to eat grass around the place. He wanted to find horses but this was a good place to stop awhile and graze.

A little to the north of this green valley grew clumps of pine trees, and off at a distance to the west could be seen a small stream winding lazily along through thin belts of willow and cottonwood. Cinchfoot was quietly eating grass when all of a sudden he heard the pounding of hoofs, which he recognized as those of a running horse. He saw a horse rush from behind the pine trees on the west. It was Blaze Face himself, coming on at a run! Cinchfoot did not have time to wonder. He looked just in time to see a rider behind Blaze Face, and the rider quickly stopped his horse. He had seen Cinchfoot. And the next instant Cinchfoot was running hard with Blaze Face. They rushed on toward the south while the lone cowboy sat his horse and looked.

He had stopped his horse the moment he saw Cinchfoot. It was such a big surprise he could hardly believe it. He did not know where Blaze Face and Cinchfoot had been for so long a time. And neither he nor Cinchfoot knew that Blaze Face, when he had escaped that day, had made his way around the canyon and up to this place over the same route Cinchfoot had come. But it did not matter how it had happened. It had happened and that was enough. There would be a vast amount of running to do now on the part of Cinchfoot and the cowboys, but as yet only this lone rider knew that Cinchfoot had come back and that lone rider was Clem Brown.

Clem turned his horse and rode hard toward the ranch. It was evening when he arrived. All the other riders had come in already. Clem pulled up his sweating horse near a score of cowboys. The riders all stood looking at him, knowing in the language of the range that "somethin' was up." Clem dismounted, pulled the saddle from his puffing horse and said, "I saw Cinchfoot today, big as life! Blaze Face is with him. I want you fellers to get all the saddle horses rounded up

and keep 'em ready. As soon as we locate
Cinchfoot again we'll start for him. I aim to
take the whole outfit out there and run him
down. And it'll take the whole outfit to do it
—you can bet plenty!"

XIV : *Fighting Gray Wolves*

CLEM BROWN was doomed to disappointment, not only the next day but for months afterward. Blaze Face and Cinchfoot had run far into the wild places, and Blaze Face had not the slightest notion of ever coming back. And because Cinchfoot hated men generally, and all their ways, all men except Clem Brown, he was willing to go into the wildest country, with Blaze Face leading. All Cinchfoot thought of was that he wanted to be free and do as he pleased. He had not the slightest notion what kind of country Blaze Face was running toward and likely Blaze Face didn't know either. All that old Blaze Face wanted was a place so wild and far away from all men that neither he nor Cinchfoot would ever be seen again. And so it was that Blaze Face led on day after day, for many days, with Cinchfoot following until, in a far distant region, Blaze Face stopped one day, and here it seemed was a good place to stay.

It was September. All went well for some weeks. It was not until the middle of October that Blaze Face and Cinchfoot came upon some other horses. These were range horses that had escaped from men and, liking the wild, wanted to stay away. There were only ten of these half wild range horses but they were hardy and as determined to live and fight their way as were Cinchfoot and Blaze Face. The range horses nickered in a friendly way as soon as they saw the two big black horses. They all wanted company.

By the middle of November the nights were very cold and when December came a foot of snow fell. The north wind rushed and howled through the valleys and across the ridges to freeze living things that did not find shelter. Each night the small band of hardy horses found shelter in a dark pine woods that dipped down from a mountainside and spread out a little distance on the valley. But even in the woods the snow was above the horses' knees and all through the long nights they stood huddled together, in misery from cold and hunger.

Each day they moved out on the valley and began the hard work of pawing down through the snow to the dead grass. This dead grass was all the horses could get to eat but it kept them alive. Cattle did not have enough intelligence to paw away the snow and so get to the grass and keep from starving. Horses were more intelligent and some horses knew more than others, and it happened that Cinchfoot and his little band were equal to any danger that was at all possible for horses to conquer in the wild.

Until February the worst danger they had to face was the cold and the hunger. As yet they had only to fight to keep from freezing during the night, and to paw down through the snow for the grass in the daytime. By the middle of February they were all thin and ill-looking. The hair on their coats was long and harsh. Even Cinchfoot's once fine black coat and great silver mane and tail all looked sorry indeed. The horses looked hollow-eyed but there was also in their eyes a light that told of determination, a kind of never-give-up look. They were the kind, each one of them, that would fight, and fight anything to save their lives, and by common consent they followed the lead of Cinchfoot.

It was late one night in February. Cinchfoot, Blaze Face and the others of the little band of horses had taken shelter from the knifing wind in a small pine woods in a low valley. Directly north of them, only a few yards, lay a mass of granite boulders, partly covered with snow. The night was clear with moon and stars shining. The biting north wind blew sullenly through the pine trees and over the mass of rocks to the rear of the horses. Cinchfoot and the other horses stood very close together, as usual, and waited miserably until the daylight should come.

Suddenly every horse raised his head and listened. One wild, weird howl sounded in the night, the howl of a timber wolf. Three times, at intervals thereafter, it sounded, then nothing could be heard but the sounds of the bitter wintry wind blowing through the tall pine trees. But every horse had heard and every horse kept his head up, alert, watching, listening.

The minutes dragged. Then, without the slightest warning, six timber wolves crashed out of the woods a few yards away and were upon the small band of horses. The trick of the timber wolf was to hamstring a horse, or cut the tendons of the hind leg, and so make the horse helpless. But the wolves had met their match here. As the starving, and therefore desperate, wolves drove in for the hind legs of their supposed victims, the heels of the horses began to fly and by a streak of good luck two wolves were killed at the first rush, both having their skulls crushed by the terrific kicks of four of the horses. While this was taking place Cinchfoot and Blaze Face each got a bad slash on their hind legs but both wounds were high, in the flesh, and no harm was done except to cause pain.

And now the place was a whirlwind of

fighting horses and wolves. Each drove hard to attack the other. The four remaining wolves rushed in with the same desperate abandon as at first. Blaze Face leaped toward one of the gray beasts and struck at it with a big front hoof but at the same time he stumbled in the rocks and fell to his knees. For a second Blaze Face was down and in that second a huge wolf leaped upon his back and slashed him once savagely, and at that instant a queer thing happened. Cinchfoot was, at the moment, right beside Blaze Face. The wolf was so close to Cinchfoot it brushed him as it leaped for Blaze Face. Seeing the wolf fairly under his nose, Cinchfoot, with mouth open, dived for the wolf, seized it at the back of the head and with his inch-and-a-half-long teeth crunched down until the bones cracked. Wild with the spirit of battle, Cinchfoot reared up and shook the wolf as a dog would shake a rat, then dropped the beast dead at his feet. At the same time Blaze Face got up and struck at another wolf with a front hoof and missed. Then all the horses leaped out and charged the three remaining wolves who had started to escape them, but one, with a broken shoulder, was caught by the horses and they squealed in their rage as they stomped the beast to a pulp in the snow.

Brief and fortunate as the battle had been, it had done some hurt also. Every horse had one or more wounds, some of them severe, and one horse had all but been hamstrung. The teeth of the wolf had missed the tendon but cut a very deep gash in the flesh. When morning came there was blood on the snow and part of it was from the horses' wounds, including those of both Cinchfoot and Blaze Face. They snorted loudly at the sight of the dead beasts around them.

Were there more of these creatures in this territory? And was there a region far distant from this place where this danger would not come? And was there a place where one could find all he wanted to eat and plenty of clear running water to drink?

Cinchfoot wanted to leave this place far behind and when it was broad day the horses moved away. All that day the horses followed Cinchfoot and it was very plain to them he was going away from this region. At times they stopped to paw the snow from the grass but they traveled on in an almost straight direction all day. The next day it was the same and the next day and for days afterward. Cinchfoot traveled on.

Did Cinchfoot know where the direction of Clem Brown's ranch was? Possibly he did. In any case he held to that general direction and when again the springtime came to the land and there was green grass and running water in all the little creeks and draws, Cinchfoot was actually in the old territory where he had been born. Only Blaze Face had come this far with him. The other horses had stopped far back. This place suited Cinchfoot, but old Blaze Face was plainly suspicious. Now and then, while chewing a big mouthful of green grass, he would come walking quickly up to Cinchfoot and look at him as if he might have said, "My good pal, have you any idea where we are? Have you, by any chance, considered that we're right back in that place where 'fellers' is and where they likely will be out here looking for us?"

But Cinchfoot paid no attention. He was very well contented. He did not even think of being hunted here. Instinctively he knew he could run. He was so well satisfied that he did no more than look around at the hills and ridges, now and then, then go on eating the green grass.

One morning, about the middle of the forenoon, Clem, by chance, was the first cowboy in that neighborhood to see Cinchfoot and Blaze Face, and as Clem said afterward, "My heart sure skipped a beat when I knowed I was looking on Cinchfoot again!" Clem was behind some pine trees on a little knoll when he looked down on the narrow valley and saw Cinchfoot with his new jet black spring coat and his glorious silver mane and tail. Clem said under his breath, "Now this is one time when he won't get away. If horses and fellers ever made a run, then we'll run him down and we'll tackle that job in the morning and we'll fix it so, no matter how long he runs, there'll be more horses to throw in when the first ones gets tired."

As Clem lay in the shelter watching, he wanted Cinchfoot so much it was hard to go back to the ranch, miles away, and get ready for the next day. Clem said to himself, "Did anybody ever see a purtier horse than he is? It would be awful if I missed him this time because I might never get another chance. But I'll get every feller on the ranch and we'll come in from the south. With twenty good riders and lots of fresh horses led behind the wagon to use as needed, I don't see how he can ever get away. I had no chance to try to run him down the other time. He was gone when that day come but as yet I don't think anybody but me has seen him. And I don't see any feller in sight anywhere to scare him. And anyway, every feller understands that even if he *does* see him, he's to get away quick and easy as possible and tell *me*. So things look purty good."

Clem led his horse carefully down the slope on the other side where he could not be seen when he rode away at a fast gallop, disappearing in the distance toward the ranch house.

XV: *A Man and His Horse*

IT was two hours after sunrise that morning when Clem and his whole outfit of cowboys came riding across the valleys and ridges toward the west. Clem and Sam Blades had been scouting the place and had learned that both Cinchfoot and Blaze Face were in this vicinity. Clem had watched them through field glasses. As the cowboys rode out this morning to try to run Cinchfoot down they were prepared. A wagon trailed along behind with other horses tied at the back and no riders on them. These would be used when the horses on which the men now rode would be fagged out, chasing Cinchfoot.

The cowboys, Clem at the head of them, rode in a group, and when they were close to the place where Cinchfoot and Blaze Face had been seen, not much was said. The only sounds were those of the horses' hoofs thump-

ing on the ground, the squeaking of the saddles
and, now and then, some low word spoken by
a cowboy. These were all good riders and they
were mounted on good horses, too. But none
of the riders were deceived about Cinchfoot.
They knew that not only the horses they rode
but all the others trailing behind the wagon
would have to give everything they had to
catch Cinchfoot. And they would be lucky
even at that, if they got him. As to old Blaze
Face, Clem had said when they started out this
morning, "Now, fellers, pay no attention to
old Blaze Face. He's old now and likely we'll
run him down, but let him alone on account
he'll sure come home to stay if we can rope
Cinchfoot and take him in."

The cowboys reached the foot of a low ridge
and, as it happened, they were all abreast as
they rode up to the top of the ridge. Suddenly
every horse's ears went forward and his eyes
got wider at what he saw down on the valley
just below. There was a second of tense silence, then Clem yelled, "There he is!" Instantly, every rider spurred his mount and

horses and men raced down the low hill, Clem ahead of them all.

Cinchfoot and Blaze Face, grazing together, had looked up suddenly to see the many riders on the ridge. One swift look and Cinchfoot whirled and thundered away toward the west, his great jet black body shining in the morning sun, his beautiful silver mane and tail streaming in the wind. Blaze Face, for a time, kept close behind but it was seen by Clem that Cinchfoot was running easily while Blaze Face was doing his very best from the start. Straight into the west lay a wide level plain. Cinchfoot led the cavalcade of horsemen behind him. One mile, two, three, five, and now all the horses were sweating and some of them puffing. But Cinchfoot seemed hardly to be warmed up. He would run swiftly some distance ahead of Blaze Face, then stop and look back, his proud head held high, his beauty like some great picture of a magnificent horse. For a few seconds he would stand and wait until Blaze Face got closer, then away he would run again, throwing his high head from side to side, and he seemed thrilled at all this because he had no notion that these cowboys could ever get closer to him than they were at present.

But Clem was crafty and his cowboys had their instructions. They must not try to push the race at first, just run their horses hard enough to keep well in sight of Cinchfoot. If Cinchfoot should increase his speed then Clem and the others would do the same. And at first Cinchfoot was so sure of himself that he played into Clem's hands without knowing it. If Cinchfoot had understood, he would at once have run as fast as he could and so have escaped. But he took his time and ran easily. When ten miles had been run, even with Cinchfoot slowing down and trotting now and then, he began to be a little concerned about Blaze Face. He started out, Clem said, "to run plumb away," and he could have done so if it had not been for Blaze Face, but that old horse couldn't run now as he did when he was the age of Cinchfoot. At one time Cinchfoot cut loose with a great burst of speed but

Blaze Face could go no faster. Another five miles was covered and it was the same. Then as the race went on Cinchfoot could see that unless Blaze Face could hurry faster, things would be bad. He raced away again and ran a mile with amazing speed, stopped, looked back and nickered for Blaze Face to hurry. But it was no use. Old Blaze Face was getting farther behind.

At last something happened to confuse Cinchfoot. He saw Blaze Face, who was far behind, turn and run toward the south. But the half dozen cowboys on that side paid no attention to him. Clem had told them what to do if this happened. They let him go past them and rode as hard toward Cinchfoot as ever. And all of them were now on fresh horses. Cinchfoot decided now to run away. He increased his speed and so ran for two miles. Then it seemed to him it would be better to run harder still and so get clear out of sight. Away he went this time as fast as he could but to his anxiety the riders did not seem to fall far behind him. Mile after mile the race went on. Cinchfoot was now sweating and splotches of foam were showing on his once sleek, black coat. He was breathing hard for the first time but he was still sure he could get away. Still on and on, and on still he ran and at last the vast level plain that seemed to have no end was almost maddening. His breathing was becoming harder and harder. If he could only find some friendly ravine or even a clump of timber to run in and somehow shake off these persistent men. Far to the west, the direction in which he was running, he could see the high peaks of the mountains and the foothills below, covered with vast pine forests. Cinchfoot did not know exactly what was in that dark, distant silence but he knew instinctively that if he could get there he might find a friendly place to hide in and so get away. He did not know that Clem, the crafty one, had waited patiently until the race could be run in this particular place. Cinchfoot only knew that if he got away he must run as he had never run before.

When he saw the mountain peaks with the

forest in the distance he forgot Blaze Face,
forgot everything except the hard-riding men
behind him and that he must reach the dark
forest in the distance. He kept his eyes di-
rected there. Once he passed a tall lone pine
out in the valley. No place to hide there. Then
he was aware that one of the men was riding
away off to one side. And the rider seemed to
be already far ahead of the others. This man
was now riding south of Cinchfoot and keeping almost even with him and then Cinchfoot
saw that the man was getting ahead of him on
that side, yet he did not come any closer.
What was that rider trying to do? Cinchfoot
did not know that the lone rider riding so hard
off there to the south was the best friend
Cinchfoot ever had known; of course Cinchfoot *couldn't* know this. He didn't know the
rider was Clem Brown and that as this race
had gone on, Clem had looked through his
field glasses and seen how the black coat of
Cinchfoot was splashed with foam. And
Cinchfoot didn't know how miserable Clem
felt as he urged his horse to go faster off there

to the south—urged him to go faster so that the great beautiful black horse, with the silver mane and tail, wouldn't run his heart out. Long before, Clem knew how bad all this was; no one could know better than Clem. Five times, in this race, the men had changed to fresh horses, and incredible as it seemed, Cinchfoot was still running. And only Clem knew, and almost felt, the hard breaths that Cinchfoot now had to fight for.

As Clem rode on he talked and complained to himself, "Daggone it all. It's awful to do this to him, but he'll never come in and he'll never know unless I once get him. It's for him I'm doing this, but he can't understand." All the other riders knew where Clem was going. It had been arranged among them. It would still take Clem some time to get where he wanted to go, but he would be there and ready when the time came.

In the far West, things that are far away look very near. Distances are so deceiving there. Cinchfoot didn't know this. He knew only that the mountains and the trees off there in the west seemed to stay the same distance away no matter how hard he ran. He did not know that Clem was on a fresh horse, the fifth one for him in this race. He only knew that the rider off there to the south was far ahead.

The rather slow going of both Cinchfoot and Blaze Face at the beginning had taken up a lot of time. Hours had gone by at this time, and it was well along in the afternoon. And what made Clem anxious was that the last of the horses that had any wind left in them were now being used. Unless some trick could be used, it seemed possible Cinchfoot might still run every horse down and get away. It seemed impossible, yet there was Cinchfoot running still! Clem put the long-legged bay he was riding to his best pace. He must reach a certain clump of trees where he wanted to hide. It would take a lot of the wind out of Clem's horse to get to it but there was no other way. Clem figured that if his trick failed he might still be able to run up on Cinchfoot with this last horse.

On and on Clem urged his horse and at last

he reached the little grove of pine trees out on
the plain not far from the foothills. Into this
little grove he rode his horse and there he sat
on the puffing mount and waited, waited with
his coiled rope ready.

Cinchfoot was coming. Yes! there he was,
coming straight toward this little grove. The
riders were coming too—coming and spurring
their jaded mounts, but spur as they would
they were falling farther and farther behind.
And even in the distance Clem saw that
Cinchfoot was in a bad way. Surely, Clem
thought, he could ride suddenly out of the
grove and throw his loop over Cinchfoot.
Clem was skillful with a rope. Surely he
wouldn't miss! But to Clem's disgust, as he
sat here looking at the great black horse
coming on, he found himself trembling like
a leaf. He scolded himself, saying he must
not get excited and so miss with his rope, but
his hands kept trembling, something unusual
for Clem Brown.

Nearer and nearer the unsuspecting Cinchfoot came, fighting with all the heart in him,

fighting to the last to be free. Above everything else in his life he wanted to be free—
free all his days, for he could think of but one
thing while these men raced behind him. This
was what had happened to him while he was
with the rodeo—where he had been a prisoner
those long years with the hard treatment at
the hands of the men who rode him. Cinchfoot was now in so desperate a situation he did
not even think of Blaze Face and could think
of nothing but trying to fight on. Things were
beginning to quiver before his eyes—the
mountain peaks, the forests, the ground only a
little beyond—Cinchfoot could no longer see
the ground clearly. Sharp pains were in his
chest as he fought for breath, and his legs
trembled with weakness at every leap he took,
and every leap now was made not because his
flesh was willing but because, even as his mind
began to grow dim, he wanted to be free from
men.

For a second Clem saw it all—saw Cinchfoot only a few yards away and Clem understood everything. He urged his horse forward

and shot out from his hiding place in the little grove. Clem's coiled rope was on his arm. He cast the loop. Cinchfoot suddenly stopped. The rope fell harmless on his nose. Cinchfoot again ran on. Clem saw the once beautiful black coat of Cinchfoot covered with sweat and foam and he was so close he could see the heaving sides; he saw the bloodshot, suffering eyes, saw the dilated nostrils with the blood dripping from them, heard the groaning breath of Cinchfoot as he fought to the last to be free.

In that brief time Clem felt as bad as Cinchfoot. And all the other riders were far away, but coming slowly on their spent horses. And Cinchfoot was still going free. At first Clem's horse, urged on by the quirt, seemed to gain a little but, to Clem's astonishment, Cinchfoot still raced on. If he should escape now he might never be seen again, probably would fall and die in some wild, lonely place. Clem shouted to his mount and hit him hard with the quirt in an effort to get up to Cinchfoot and again try to throw the rope over his head. But it was no use. Impossible as it seemed, Cinchfoot was keeping the distance between him and Clem, and surely, unless he got help here the great Cinchfoot would escape.

Clem was once again almost near enough to throw his rope, almost, but not quite. For a long minute it seemed to him that surely it must soon be over, surely Cinchfoot, only a little ahead, must go down under the strain. Clem was so close he again saw the foam-covered body, and riding a little to one side, as he was, he saw again the heaving sides of Cinchfoot as he fought for breath, saw the eyes that were rimmed with the alkali dust and heard the loud groaning breathing, and again he saw the quivering nostrils and blood coming from them. Surely now it must end. But still the minutes dragged, and still the fearful pace went on. And then to Clem's amazement he saw that slowly, very slowly, the distance was widening between him and Cinchfoot!

Trembling with the tension, Clem whipped

his horse unmercifully. He hardly knew what he was doing. Some power seemed to grip him and he whipped his tiring horse now as if the life of Cinchfoot depended on it. Clem's horse with every jump pounded the sod with his hoofs hard and every jump brought a labored groan from the horse. Only once Clem seemed to remember that other riders had been in this race, and once he turned for a quick look to the rear. To his bewilderment he saw the riders back, far back. It seemed to Clem they had deserted him. But no, he knew that they had not done that. The last horses had given all they had and they hadn't had enough. All kinds of thoughts raced through Clem's mind. He would never get Cinchfoot now unless some help came. His own horse was fighting, puffing and groaning and giving all he had but this could not last. Why wouldn't Cinchfoot give up, quit, stand still? It would all be so easy and then he could have everything he wanted. But it was not nature's way. Cinchfoot struggled on because he didn't understand. He did not know what to do now but to fight on

and on, even to his death it might be. Clem
used his whip and even struck his jaded horse
desperately with the coiled rope, but it was
still the same; Cinchfoot seemed to gain only
inches but surely he was gaining a little.

The crimson sun hung low in the west. The
long plain ahead, the scattering pines, all were
strangely still. It seemed that nature herself
was hushed by the sight of the great, fighting,
groaning, foam-covered horse.

All at once a long slope of ground lay
ahead. Less than a mile beyond this shelving
ground stood a pine forest which covered that
side of the valley and stretched far up the
foothills into the peaks of the Rockies. Clem
saw and he knew. Cinchfoot was fighting
desperately to reach the pine forest. If he
could do that he could surely escape in the
friendly shelter of the forest. And after that
the wildest places farther west would be ready
to receive him, and again he could roam in
the vast wild freedom with no man's hand
upon him. That there was one man who might
make the tame world more to be desired than

all this Cinchfoot did not know. He had forgotten that man, and if he escaped here there
might be nothing ever again to call up those
memories.

And now a strange thing happened. Nature
in the West is a queer thing. She may help or
she may destroy and she is not partial to man
or horse. Halfway down the long incline was
the beginning of a small arroyo that led to a
stream out in the valley. This arroyo began
with a short drop, not more than two feet, but
the drop was a sheer one. And here it was that
nature herself, and not the plans of man,
made possible the capture of Cinchfoot. Fighting with every ounce of strength in him he all
at once reached the head of the small arroyo.
He tried to leap sidewise and avoid it but at
last his exhausted body would no longer re-
spond to this extra effort. He stumbled and
went down into the arroyo and for the time
his senses left him. He lay with his head on
the ground, his body partly in the shallow
arroyo. Clem rode up, leaped from his heaving horse and stood over Cinchfoot. Cinch-

foot's bloodshot eyes looked glazed, his great sides rose and fell and he did not try to move.

Clem's hands trembled as he carefully tied his long rope around Cinchfoot's neck and then as carefully tied one hind foot, but that was all. Clem was standing and looking down at Cinchfoot when all the other cowboys rode up. Clem told them to keep pretty well back and bring some water up from the small stream in the valley.

Presently several hatfuls of water were brought. One hatful was handed to Clem and then the men all got well back and sat on the ground as Clem had told them to do. Cinchfoot raised his head. Clem was talking low to him, scratching his neck and calling him by his colt name, Blackie. Then to all the men sitting a little away and looking, a surprising thing happened. They saw that Cinchfoot was drinking water from the big hat Clem held to his nose. They saw Cinchfoot prick up his ears and look at them. And when he saw them he kicked out one hind leg, the one the rope was on, as if he was going to fight to get away. But although he kept staring at the men, he made no other move. Clem held the two ropes in his hand and all the time he kept talking low to Cinchfoot, still calling him by his baby name, Blackie. And Clem kept on talking to him as he did back in the old corral. Clem knew Cinchfoot was still starving for water but he knew also that this must be given to him slowly.

Sam Blades said afterward it was because Cinchfoot was "so daggoned winded he just couldn't get up here that he didn't fight." As to why he did not try to fight cannot be known. But likely Sam was wrong, for when Clem brought out the small yellow sack with brown sugar and said, "Sugar, Blackie, want some? Sugar! It's good!" Cinchfoot smelled of it a little and then licked it from the palm of Clem's hand just as he did long ago when Clem used to feed him the sugar and make a fuss over him. He was only a baby in age then but now he was a horse in middle age.

More than an hour went by with Cinchfoot resting here. Clem, still holding to the ends of

the two ropes, walked back for more hatfuls of water until it was best not to give more.
Then it was seen that Cinchfoot was going to
try to get up. He put his front legs out in
front of him. He tried once, then seemed to
think he would rest a little first, and he did.
Meanwhile he kept pricking his ears forward
and looking at the men and their puffing
horses a little away.

Clem all this time kept scratching Cinchfoot's neck and talking to him. Presently
Cinchfoot tried to get up again and this time
he got up on all four feet. He looked a little
anxiously toward the men sitting quietly on
the ground a short distance away and when
they made no move he put his nose down to
Clem who was again offering some sugar and
saying, "Sugar, Blackie. It's good, come and
eat it." Cinchfoot licked it up from Clem's
hand but as he did this he kept watching the
men.

Clem now walked carefully, moving very
slowly to his own horse, and tied the rope
that was on Cinchfoot's neck to the saddle

horn. Then he took some time to get the loop from Cinchfoot's hind foot. Now came the big test. Would Cinchfoot follow Clem if Clem led him? Clem swung into his saddle and started, started very slowly, pulled a little on the rope, and said, "Come on, Blackie! Sugar!"

The men, all waiting tensely, saw Clem start riding away and Cinchfoot following. He kept so close to Clem on the horse that Cinchfoot's nose was very close to Clem's knee. The other cowboys rode some little distance behind.

It was far into the night when they reached the ranch house. Clem led Cinchfoot into a corral that he could have all to himself. Clem scratched his neck for a time and water was brought for Cinchfoot to drink. And after some time Clem and the cowboys went to the ranch house for the rest of the night. Although they all slept soundly they awakened early, as was their custom, a little before sunup. They noticed that Clem's bunk was empty. So he was already outside.

The men came out and found a surprise. Out on the prairie some distance away they saw Clem with his hand up to Cinchfoot's nose and Cinchfoot was, as the cowboys said, "plumb loose." There was no rope on him. They knew something had gone wrong. Clem, seeing them, called out, "Bring a rope! Don't come too close. Lay it on the ground and then you fellers keep back!"

This was done. Clem started slowly toward the rope on the ground, talking all the while to Cinchfoot, and Cinchfoot made low friendly sounds close to Clem. When they reached the rope, Clem stooped down slowly and picked it up and very, very slowly moved his hand up and over Cinchfoot's neck and the rope was soon tied. Then while the others looked on he stood proudly looking at them.

When he had led Cinchfoot to the corral where the gate was open, he stopped suddenly. Everyone heard a wild piercing nicker off toward the west. They all looked in that direction. It was old Blaze Face coming at a run! He raced up to within fifty yards and snorted.

Cinchfoot's eyes shone with eagerness. He began to nicker to Blaze Face but Cinchfoot did not seem excited now. He was calling calmly to his old friend. And pretty soon Cinchfoot seemed to know that Blaze Face had come up to stay, for he quit nickering to him and he put his nose down close to Clem and in horse talk asked Clem for some more brown sugar. Clem led him on into the corral and asked the cowboys to shut the gate. They did this and Sam Blades said, "What happened, Clem?"

Clem replied, "That gate came open. I was sure I shut it good but I guess I didn't and when I came outside my heart was in my mouth. The gate was open and Cinchfoot was grazing out about a quarter of a mile as free as a bird. I called to him, telling him I had some of that same sugar, and he trotted right up to me in no time and began to talk in his way, saying, 'Well, Clem, if you've got some of that sweetening, give it to me!' And as he came up he was also saying as plain as day, 'That gate came open in the night and I could have left you permanent but I wouldn't leave poor old Clem!'"

The cowboys were all perched on top of the corral looking at Clem and Cinchfoot. Sam Blades grinned and said, "It was the brown sugar made him stay."

Clem grinned happily. He said, "Only a little of it was the sugar. He practically told me as much!"

Blaze Face had come up near the corral. He was looking around and putting his nose to the ground and snorting at things generally. Clem grinned more than ever. He said, "Old Blaze Face won't ever be rode again. He can rest from now on but he don't know it. He is doing as he is now, by way of talking to Cinchfoot. He's maybe saying to him, 'Oh, well, of course if *you're* that set on that feller I reckon I'll have to stay here too. But I give notice that while I ain't as young as I used to be, if they think I ain't got any buck left in me, why, I'll show 'em they're mistaken.'"

Cinchfoot looked out once at Blaze Face trotting about here and there, smelling things and snorting at them. And Cinchfoot went on calmly licking sugar from Clem's hand. Clem said, "Cinchfoot is thinking, 'I'm not troubled about the way my friend is doing out there. That's just his way of trying to make fellers think he's plumb disgusted!'" And Clem added, "Facts are Blaze Face can hardly wait till time for his oats. He's only putting on a little act and he's plumb happy to be back here with Cinchfoot."